Sherlock Holmes and The Cornwall Affair

By Johanna M. Rieke

Paperback ISBN 978-1-78705-549-0
ePub ISBN 978-1-78705-550-6
PDF ISBN 978-1-78705-551-3

MX Publishing
335 Princess Park Manor, Royal Drive,
London, N11 3GX
www.mxpublishing.com

Cover design by Brian Belanger
Translation by Bryan Stone

For Lisa and Bryan, who both shared with me their great
love of Cornwall

At the Diogenes Club

It was, as I recall, on a rainy morning in the last week in September, in the year 1890, that the adventure began, which I would now, dear reader, like to recount to you. I had not seen my friend Sherlock Holmes since our return together from Switzerland. I was therefore surprised to receive a letter from him, telling me that he was invited the same afternoon to a discussion with his brother, Mycroft Holmes, at Mycroft's club, and that if I could be there he would value my presence. The prospect of seeing my old friend again was most tempting. During lunch with my dear wife, Mary, I told her of Holmes' letter and told her of my decision to accept the invitation. In wise forethought, that I might well be rather late home, I suggested that she should not expect me for dinner.

As soon as I had left my practice in Kensington, I embarked upon my daily round of visits. Since London seemed to be suffering an endless grey autumn, marked by steady rain and low temperatures, all of my patients seemed to be suffering heavy colds. Most, however, seemed well on the way to recovery. And indeed, as I observed, with some relief, that the last patient of the day was responding well to my treatment, I was able, with some relief, first to attend to an urgent private matter, and then to take up Holmes' invitation. I was expected at the Diogenes Club at five o'clock, and as I saw that time was slipping away faster than I thought, I was very relieved to find a free hansom cab. A lively trot led us to Pall Mall, where the Diogenes Club stands a short distance from the Carlton Theatre. In the case, respected reader, that you do not know this establishment, I may here assure you that the Diogenes Club is the most unusual club in London, perhaps indeed in the Kingdom. Its members lay such great store upon their peace and their private affairs, that conversation, even between members, is not tolerated. Visitors may only enter the Strangers' room; there a discreet conversation with a club member may take place. Sherlock Holmes once told me that the Diogenes Club counted among its members certainly the most unsociable and, for a club, the unlikeliest Londoners. Indeed, dear reader, you may well ask whether there might not then be a better place than precisely this club, for the Holmes brothers to meet and talk.

To answer the question, it behoves me first to tell you a little about Mycroft Holmes. He is seven years older than his brother, and by comparison with Holmes' slender and athletic figure, he might better be described as stout. The two brothers are, however, in various respects similar; both have the same watchful eyes, the same prominent nose, and the same high forehead that marks a deep thinker. Both possess a highly developed power of observation, and an extraordinary gift for drawing logical conclusions. Sherlock Holmes once told me that this ability was in reality much more highly developed in Mycroft than in himself. Mycroft Holmes could however never have exercised, as did his brother, the profession of consulting detective. The explanation lies in the very different personalities of the two brothers. As I had in my own experience occasion to confirm, Sherlock Holmes led a very erratic life, whereas that of his brother was marked by calm and order. Mycroft Holmes is a member of the civil service, and spends his day mostly in Whitehall. During the time from a quarter to five to twenty past seven, he is to be found at the Diogenes Club, directly opposite his private dwelling. Apart from these fixed times, he appears to have no private interests. In case that appears to you very singular, and difficult to envisage, it may, dear reader, help you to know that Sherlock Holmes assures me that his brother, in all discretion, and, far from being simply something important in the government, is in fact the government. You will therefore well understand that in these circumstances the Diogenes Club surely presents the best place for a conversation with Mycroft Holmes. And I was to have the privilege of taking part. As I leaned back in my hansom, I looked forward eagerly to the meeting with the two brothers, and tried to imagine what Mycroft Holmes might wish to share with us.

It was just after five o'clock, as I paid the cabman and hastened into the club building. I gave my name and my business, and my coat and doctor's bag were taken from me, as I was shown into the Strangers' room. All was completely correct and clearly executed, as the staff of this house of quiet are accustomed also to conduct themselves without words.

On entering the room, I found the brothers sitting by the fireplace. Both rose to greet me. We then took our places, and after a moment's pause while whisky and smoking materials were brought, Sherlock Holmes spoke, somewhat reproachfully, to me. "I had begun to think you were not coming, Watson. You are usually a model of punctuality."

Before I could offer any explanation, Mycroft Holmes remarked: "Perhaps his personal business on the way took longer than he expected."

Puzzled, I looked at him closely, as his brother again took up the word: "And his round of patients' visits, which he completed beforehand."

I looked at once in surprise at my friend. Before I could say anything, however, Mycroft Holmes again made a further observation. "And then there was the unplanned visit to a corner shop."

Puzzled and disagreeably disturbed, I looked from one brother to the other. They had described, precisely, what I had done since lunch. How could they? Had someone followed me? But why, and how? Finally I caught my breath and asked them both, somewhat irritated:

"But how do you know how I have spent my afternoon?"

"That was not especially difficult," answered Holmes, and continued in his relaxed manner. "Your pocket notebook, in which you keep your written notes on your patients, is at first always in your left-hand jacket pocket. When your round is complete, you transfer the notebook to your right-hand jacket pocket, where it is now. And as you are a conscientious doctor, you completed your round before doing anything else"

I looked with surprise at Holmes, who only drew contentedly on his pipe, while now his brother continued to astonish me.

"Concerning the personal business, you have a receipt from a watchmaker in the Strand in your jacket pocket. I suggest that you have had your watch cleaned, or repaired. Frodsham & Co. are well known in London for their excellent services in such matters"

"Quite," added Sherlock Holmes, and continued: "Moreover, you usually wear your watch-chain rather differently. That clearly indicates haste in arranging it with your watch newly attached."

Before I could react, Mycroft was again already speaking. "And then there is the broken shoelace. Your left foot clearly landed in a deep puddle, for the shoe is, compared to the other, still wet. You have taken that shoe off to shake out the water. As you put it on again, the shoelace broke. You went quickly into a shop to buy a new one, and threaded it yourself, while you were in the hansom cab in which you arrived."

I looked at Mycroft Holmes again in amazement. He had perfectly described what happened, but how did he know that I had not called on a shoe repairer? And how did he know about the hansom? I asked him, and the reply was immediate. "First, the hansom: just before you arrived, Dr. Watson, the rain was very heavy. Had you come on foot, your trousers and jacket, and overcoat, must have been soaked. So you took a hansom. Now, back to the shoelace: it is threaded, in contrast to your other shoe, backwards. That would not occur in a shoe-shop or gentlemen's outfitters. There remains only the explanation of the general store, which, I understand, is to be found today on practically every street corner of our city. You were in a hurry, so you decided to change the lace yourself in the safety of your dry hansom. Alas, although a hansom may be very agile in negotiating in the congested London traffic, it is still rather narrow. You had to thread your shoelace more by touch than by sight. The consequence is apparent; you have two differently threaded shoes".

Somewhat embarrassed, I looked at my shoes, and then in the expressionless features of the two brothers. On the one hand it was fascinating to follow this example of the acuity of their observation, On the other hand it was not agreeable to be so analysed. It was therefore a relief, when Mycroft spoke again, to say: "But we must put an end to this amusement, and pursue the real purpose of this meeting."

Mycroft Holmes explains

The conversation which follows, I give to you, as far as my memory permits, word for word.

"Before I enter further into the details, I must first remind you, that everything which I now tell you must be treated with the utmost discretion." With a nod I gave my agreement with Mycroft Holmes' words. A glance at my friend Sherlock Holmes told me that he had closed his eyes and now held his fingertips together. His face showed no expression, but as his friend of long standing I knew that his attention was now fully concentrated on that which his brother would say. Mycroft obviously recognised this behaviour, and so he addressed his remarks directly to me.

"Dr. Watson, does the name Thomas Charles Reginald Agar-Robartes, second Baron Robartes of Lanhydrock and Truro, mean something to you?" Apart from a vague recollection that Truro was an important city in Cornwall, I could say nothing in reply.

"Allow me then to share with you something of the history of this most respected family. Their family record can be confirmed at least back to the sixteenth century. There is much of interest to the historians, but allow me to concentrate on the last three generations. We begin therefore with Anna Maria Hunt, a member of the female line of Robartes. In 1804 she married the London lawyer Charles Bagenal Agar. From this union ensued three sons, of whom only the second, Thomas James Agar, survived childhood. These were however not the only bereavements which Mrs Agar had to suffer. Her husband died in 1811, and so she lived alone with her son, at Lanhydrock, which came to her as an inheritance from a directly related uncle".

Here Mycroft Holmes made a short pause. I took the opportunity to pursue the conversation.

"Lanhydrock is then, I take it, the family seat of the Robartes?" "Quite so, Dr. Watson. Lanhydrock has a most varied history. It was first built as a monastery farmhouse, but with the dissolution of the monasteries under King Henry VIII, it was no longer required. A family from the neighbourhood soon claimed it and continued to cultivate it. In later years it changed hands a number of times through marriage until it came into the hands of Sir Richard Robartes, a prosperous merchant and banker from Truro. Sir Richard rebuilt the farmhouse, and his son John Robartes, in the last century, built a substantial country house. Subsequent generations preferred, however, to live outside Cornwall, and the house fell into disrepair. It was thus only when Mrs. Agar took over the property that the house was awakened to new life. Her son, who had changed his name to Agar-Robartes, supported his mother's plans and completed the rebuilding. Lanhydrock now offered him, and his wife, and their son, Thomas Charles, an adequately representative home. In 1869 he was accorded the title of first Baron of Lanhydrock and Truro. I must stress that his presence in the House of Lords reflected a most farsighted and liberal position. This is also apparent, when we consider his contribution to various charitable works, especially on behalf of the miners in his part of Cornwall. In this he was supported by his wife, Lady Juliana. But tragedy was in store. Almost ten years ago, Lanhydrock suffered a most destructive fire. Although the damage was severe, there were mercifully no immediate casualties."

Here Mycroft Holmes paused again briefly, and sipped thoughtfully at his whisky, before going on: "Sadly, Lady Juliana died within a week of this disaster, and her husband survived her by scarcely a year. The son, Thomas Charles Agar-Robartes, inherited the title. As soon as he had restored the wing of the house destroyed by the fire, he came to live with his family in Lanhydrock House. As was his father, the present Baron is a most considerate, helpful and also devout man. He has continued the charitable work of his mother, and is widely known as a friend of the poor. It is therefore no surprise, that he too is conspicuous in the House of Lords for his liberal conviction. His uncompromising commitment to the state of the needy has frequently met with the disapproval of his political opponents. If these confine themselves normally to verbal attacks, Lord Robartes has also sometimes encountered abuse and scarcely veiled threats. He can undoubtedly hold himself above such hostility, however, as he always demonstrates excellent judgment and invariably has a most favourable opinion of his fellows".

Here Mycroft Holmes made another pause, took a pinch of snuff from his tortoiseshell box, and, with a large red silk handkerchief, swept the last grains from his coat. I looked quickly across to my friend, who still sat motionless with his eyes closed. The silence seemed oppressive, and so to break it, I risked a question to Mycroft Holmes: "And the young lord is the reason why you have sought this conversation with us?" "Quite so, Dr. Watson. His Lordship informed me, during his recent visit in London that strange, indeed disturbing, things had been occurring in his neighbourhood. He would not go into detail, but his preoccupation was enough to cause me serious concern. This is all the greater because I learn that Mr William Ewart Gladstone has announced that he will visit Lanhydrock at the end of October". I interrupted Mycroft Holmes to ask, "The former Prime Minister?"

"Just so, Dr. Watson. You can now surely better understand, why I have to insist upon compete discretion."

I nodded my complete understanding of Mycroft's words. William Gladstone was, as you, dear reader, will surely be aware, Prime Minister from 1867 to 1874 and from 1880 to 1885. In the beginning he was a Conservative, but from the time of Sir Robert Peel's death he had pursued clearly liberal aims. Leading issues were for him, among others, the introduction of general education, and of a comprehensive reform of the educational system, as well as electoral and judicial reform. He also ended the sale of officers' commissions, and devoted himself to reducing the many causes of confrontation in Ireland. His plans to settle grievances of the Irish nationalist movement led finally to a division of his Liberal Party, and to the fall of his government. It could not be doubted that he had, while in office, made many enemies.

I was reflecting on this, as Mycroft spoke again, this time directly to his brother: "You would be doing me a great service, if you could devote yourself to his Lordship's concerns."

Sherlock Holmes slowly opened his eyes, and looked, apparently bored, at his brother. "You know well that the affairs of the aristocracy, and of politicians, are no concern of mine."

"That, my dear brother, I know only too well. I also know, however, that your passion is to disentangle puzzles and to solve problems. The words of Lord Robartes told me that Lanhydrock offers both." As Mycroft said this, I saw how my friend's eyes suddenly lit up, in anticipation of a worthy adventure.

"I agree. There is nothing at this moment keeping me in London, I can leave for Cornwall tomorrow or at the latest the next day". Holmes had made up his mind.

A satisfied smile lay on Mycroft's lips. As he then however turned again to me, the smile was gone, as quickly as it had come. "And you, Dr. Watson, you will surely support my brother in your usual way. My brother is sometimes a little lacking in tact and patience. It is surely so that in such a delicate matter, a calming influence such as yours will be indispensable." Somewhat embarrassed by these words, I looked first at Mycroft Holmes, and then at his brother. I had certainly not anticipated being called again, so quickly, to accompany my friend on another adventure. On the other hand, the prospect of escaping the rainy monotony of London was more than tempting. My decision was made. I turned to Sherlock Holmes and declared with enthusiasm: "It will be a pleasure to accompany you."

A journey to Cornwall

The prospect of a silent dinner in the dining room of the Diogenes Club was for Sherlock Holmes, as it was for me, sufficient reason, politely to take our leave of Mycroft Holmes. We chose instead to dine at Simpsons, as we had so often done when I had lodged in Baker Street. There would be opportunity enough to talk together, and also to plan our journey.

We had decided to leave by train on Wednesday, September 24th. We would give the impression of two gentlemen on holiday, and perhaps stay in a hotel or guesthouse near to Lanhydrock. It might however be possible to stay at Lanhydrock House as guests of Lord Robartes. Mycroft would ask his Lordship by telegraph, and advise us.

As far as my practice was concerned, it helped that our absence led into a weekend. Should we need to be away longer from London, I knew that I could rely on my neighbour, Dr. Smythe, to look to my patients. Satisfied that I had considered all aspects, I spent a most agreeable evening with Sherlock Holmes.

As I had anticipated, it was already late as I came home to Kensington. At such a late hour, I was surprised that the light was still burning in the salon. The gas light was still fully turned up. On entering the room, the reason was at once clear. My dear Mary sat sleeping in the great armchair in the window place, and her wooden stand was in front of her, with a small Gobelin in the frame, on which she had been embroidering. I smiled and watched her, before tenderly stroking her cheek. She blinked, closed her eyes again, and murmured sleepily, "I think I dozed off, John".

"I think so too, my dear. But now it is time for bed."

"Mmmh …", was all she could reply. With a smile, I lifted her and carried her up to the bedroom.

Next morning I told Mary at breakfast of my meeting with the two Holmes brothers. To my great pleasure, she had the most complete sympathy with my decision to accompany Holmes to Cornwall. She at once instructed Betsy, our housemaid, to fetch my trunk and travelling bag from the attic, and to look for my botany case for collecting leaves and flowers, my two fishing rods, and my small wicker basket, in which I carried my hooks and accessories. Amused, though rather surprised, I looked at Mary, who smiled and said, "If you wish to look convincingly like holiday guests…but now I must see that Betsy has her heart in her search"

On these words she kissed me gently and disappeared upstairs. Now I had first to call on Dr. Smythe, and then to open my practice, as usual. It was just before lunch that I received the following telegram:

"Watson - We are guests at Lanhydrock – Expect you quarter to nine tomorrow at Paddington Station. Sherlock Holmes"

Reassured, I put the telegram with my papers, attended to my day's routine and looked forward to our forthcoming journey.

Despite the animation which reigned at Paddington Station, I quickly found my friend, and with two porters attending to our baggage, we could find our train at our leisure. As we did so, Holmes informed me that we were to travel with the fastest train on this line. The "Cornishman," as it was named, had only been introduced this year. As we approached the platform, and I looked with Holmes for our reserved compartment, two porters had already stowed our baggage in the guard's van. As I had allowed myself already to be impressed by the size and beauty of our train, my attention was at once taken by the locomotive, which was most handsome, and gently hissed and gurgled to itself a little further on. I took a few paces further to see it better. It was truly an extraordinary machine and seemed to me to be bigger than those I had seen elsewhere. It was however not only the size which impressed me, but its overall appearance. The dark green paintwork highlighted most favourably the various gleaming brass plates. To complete the effect, there was a shining copper cap surrounding the mouth of the chimney, and even in the feeble light the brass safety valve mounting gleamed too. Above the great driving wheel was a large curved nameplate. Fascinated, I read the name PROMETHEUS. Holmes, who had clearly observed my interest, remarked, "All the locomotives of this type carry names, but no numbers".

That I had not erred in respect of the size, and especially the width, of our train, was at once clear, as soon as we took our seats in the compartment. Such roominess I had never seen. Then, as our journey began, it became also clear that the travelling comfort in these carriages was considerably more agreeable than in other trains. This was not to be underestimated in view of the long journey which we had before us. Holmes was sitting opposite me, and sensed my delight, for he said suddenly: "The comfort you now enjoy, you may attribute exclusively to Isambard Kingdom Brunel." Curious, I looked at my friend, and saw a satisfied smile in his expression, before he continued. "Mr Brunel was an outstanding engineer and a great pioneer. He designed bridges, viaducts and tunnels for the railway company. Already as a young man his father appointed him chief engineer in realising the father's greatest project, the great London Thames Tunnel between Wapping and Rotherhithe. This was already true pioneering, for there had never before been such a tunnel under a navigable river. Mr. Brunel also designed railway stations; Paddington Station, where our journey began, shows his handiwork. But he was a true innovator in other fields too; He conceived the dry dock in Bristol Harbour, and built great ships. Perhaps the names 'Great Western' or 'Great Britain' say something to you, my dear friend?"

"Regrettably not, Holmes."

"Well now; the 'Great Western' was in 1837 the greatest steamship in the world, and the 'Great Britain' entered service in 1843 as the first screw-driven transatlantic liner. Her hull was no longer built in wood, but was a double-hull of iron, with waterproof bulkheads. Brunel however earned his greatest distinction with the 'Great Eastern.'" My friend stopped for a moment, and looked at me. And indeed, the name of this ship was in some way familiar to me, though I could not say why. But then I recalled a newspaper headline that I had once seen. Triumphantly I replied: "With that ship the transatlantic cable was laid, so that telegraph communication, by Morse Code between the new and the old world, became a reality."

"Excellent, old friend! You have a sound memory, for that was almost twenty-five years ago."

As Sherlock Holmes was normally economical with his praise, I was delighted, and listened eagerly to his next remarks. "When the 'Great Eastern' was launched in 1852, she was, with her 19,000 gross registered tonnage, recognised as a true Leviathan. She was a steel sail and steam ship with six masts and two paddle wheels. She was able to carry four thousand passengers, and to circumnavigate the world without need to replenish her coal bunkers. Brunel could not however enjoy the fulfilment of this dream, for he died shortly before the maiden voyage, at the age of 53 years"

Here Sherlock Holmes paused, and drew contentedly upon his briar pipe, which had also to accompany him on the journey to Cornwall. I took the opportunity to ask a question which had puzzled me. "But tell me, Holmes, how is it then that you know so much about Mr. Brunel and about shipping?"

My friend replied with an expression, which seemed to sweep the horizon. "Since our stay in Switzerland, I have begun to deepen my knowledge of shipping in general, and of its strategic and economic importance, especially for our United Kingdom. In respect of Mr Brunel, I had learned more about him, as I had to investigate the mysterious disappearance of the young railway engineer, Mr. Michael Ellis."

I waited eagerly for more. This must have been one of the earlier cases from the time before we knew one another. I hoped however in vain for further details. My attempts to prompt him were quite without success. Then I remembered, that though he had told me much about Mr. Brunel, he had not yet answered my first question, why our journey this train was so comfortable and agreeable. Holmes blinked, as if he had been awakened from a short sleep. Then, with a slight smile, he replied: "You are quite right, old friend. I have let my descriptions run away with me, just as much as does my true chronicler. Back then to the subject. The Great Western Railway had charged Mr. Brunel with proposing and surveying a line of route from London to Bristol. He made two capital decisions. One was, that the track gauge should be seven feet, and a quarter inch, instead of the elsewhere already widely adopted four feet, eight and a half inches. He did this in the expectation that a broader gauge would enhance comfort at higher speeds".

Holmes stopped, in order to draw again on his pipe. I took the chance to say: "Then I can only congratulate Mr. Brunel posthumously for his initiative".

"I agree entirely, old friend, but I fear that it will not last much longer".

I looked in surprise at Holmes, as he continued: "Between the Great Western Railway, which alone used the broad gauge, and other railway companies, such as the London- and North Western Railway, there developed a fierce rivalry, a War of the Gauges. This led, as can easily be imagined, at many points to total chaos. It is really self-evident that an efficient system of transportation of goods and persons can only be achieved with a uniform track gauge. Already forty years ago, awareness was spreading, that the broad gauge could not, also for reasons of cost and space requirements, be the standard. Since then the broad gauge has been successively converted to the narrower standard gauge, although in places a temporary solution has been used, of laying a third rail. This allows trains of both gauges to be operated on the same route. You will therefore see that the decline of the broad gauge was inevitable. The broad gauge will soon be history, and, as I hear, work on the last section of the line to Cornwall, which we take today, will perhaps begin even in the next twelve months".

Holmes paused again, and searched in his small travelling case for various maps and his magnifying glass. A curious feeling had come over me, as I reflected, that the comfort I was enjoying would soon, just as I had discovered it, be no more. To change the subject, I asked Holmes a further question: "You had earlier said that Mr. Brunel took two important decisions concerning the Great Western Railway. One, as you have described, was the track gauge. What, then, was the other?"

"The line of route; he took the line through the Marlborough Downs and along the Thames Valley."

Holmes had scarcely said this, than I was struck by a doubt. I was prompted to interrupt him.

"Holmes, I am not really familiar with this part of the country, but as I recall, there are hardly any places big enough to justify building stations"

"That, Watson, is just the point. The line does not pass through places of note, and the stations required were often miles away from the nearest villages. It was however for Mr. Brunel, who wanted the quickest route to Bristol, a wise decision, especially considering the gradients which were to be overcome. He had, by the way, personally undertaken the surveying of the line. During the construction, which he supervised personally, he lived on the line, in a so-called Britzska" I looked critically at Holmes, who added: "This was a long covered wagon, of a type once used in Austria, drawn by horses, and with a canvas top to protect from the rain. In it were his camp bed, his drawing board and instruments, his plans of the route, tools and a substantial supply of cigars, for he was a committed smoker."

My picture of life in a Britzska left me feeling chilled, and I answered: "Mr. Brunel seems to have been a very remarkable man". "Very much so, Watson. It was reported that he only slept four hours each night."

Holmes spread out a large map as he said this, and began to study it with the aid of his magnifying glass. This was to me the signal that he considered our conversation ended. I therefore took up my book, which I had packed for the journey, and read for a while. My regard wandered however over and over to the window and the passing scene. After Bristol, where our locomotive was replaced during a short stop, the weather visibly improved. The landscape became increasingly romantic, even wild. In Exeter, I was prompted to reflect that a little further on, on the right-hand side, we might see the foothills of Dartmoor. That reminded me sharply of our adventure with the Hound of the Baskervilles, a memory which could not but set my pulse racing. It was some time before I felt calm again, but after Exeter the train ran first along the River Exe, with its many boats lying aground, in the river bed, as the tide was clearly out. The first fishing villages appeared, and I lain my book aside to enjoy the passing spectacle as we soon approached the sea. As I discovered the red cliffs before Dawlish, we seemed so close to the sea that the waves might at any time wash up and over the track. But they did not, and soon we sped on, turning inland, so I now lost sight of the sea. There followed several tunnels, and at Newton Abbot, where the engine was again changed, there began a steep climb, which the train slowly mastered under a conspicuous column of smoke.

It then occurred to me that I had since Exeter seen a number of apparently identical buildings, along the line. They were not signal-boxes, and I began to wonder what purpose they might serve. As if he had heard my as yet unspoken question, Holmes suddenly spoke to me.

"These buildings are pumping stations." I looked around, puzzled, and my friend went on:

"They are a further example of Mr. Brunel's initiative. He was most impressed by the concept of an atmospheric railway, and attempted to apply it to this section of the line."

"An atmospheric railway? How am I to understand that, Holmes?"

"The driving force was here to be achieved, as the name suggests, by atmospheric pressure. This worked upon a piston, which was attached to the first waggon, which served as locomotive, and which slid in a pipe between the rails, entering it through a longitudinal slit on top. In the various pumping stations which you have observed, there were steam-driven pumps which drew out the air in front of the piston, creating a vacuum, while behind it air at atmospheric pressure could enter the pipe. The difference in pressure on both sides of the piston gave the force used to pull the train."

Holmes interrupted his explanation to stuff his briar pipe again.

"That seems a most interesting idea for railway traction, Holmes. Is it still in use?"

"No, Watson, the atmospheric railway was an invention where the theory was fascinating, but the practice only brought difficulties"

Curious, I looked to Holmes as he explained further.

"Firstly, the steam engines installed were much too weak to serve their purpose. They had therefore to operate longer, and at higher speed, than was planned, and their coal consumption was excessive; the machines were not economic. On the other hand, the slit in the pipe could not be kept tight, so that traction power was lost. The reason for this was that it was provided with a leather flap to seal it, and this sealing leather had to be lubricated with cod liver oil. The lubrication with fish oil attracted rats in such a number that their hunger destroyed the leather seal, and rendered the system ineffective." With this, Holmes contentedly turned again to his pipe and concentrated on his maps, while I turned again to my book.

I would not wish, dear reader, to burden your patience by describing in detail the remainder of our journey.

Nevertheless, I feel obliged to describe that moment when we approached the crossing of the River Tamar, the border to Cornwall. Superficially the countryside around Plymouth, with its distinguished, harbour, on the east side, is not so very different from that on the west side behind Saltash. I had however an unmistakeable sensation that on leaving Devonshire, we were also leaving behind us that familiar England which I had so cherished. Deep in this thought, I found Holmes again turning towards me.

"The wide valley of the Tamar seemed at first an insuperable obstacle for the railway. Moreover, the Admiralty demanded that any bridge should be a hundred feet above high water, with depth of seventy-five feet of water, and assure a passage for navigation four hundred feet wide. It seemed to many engineers that these conditions could not be met. One engineer however took up the challenge and found a solution. His bridge was built with one pillar in deep water, and two spans, which were carried by curved tubes of elliptical section. But you can convince yourself, Watson." With these words he pointed to the window, and in that moment I caught a first view of that extraordinary and elegant bridge. I stood up quickly at the compartment door and, with the leather strap, lowered the window. I leaned out as far as I could to miss nothing of this engineering masterpiece. Behind me Holmes' monotonous voice explained that the bridge was named the Royal Albert Bridge, and that the foundations of the main pillar were built with help of a caisson, an iron cylinder in which high-pressure air prevented entry of water. I hardly heard him, for my full attention was for the bridge which we were now crossing. On the other side, a curve to the left allowed me to look back upon the bridge pillar, which formed an arch over the rails. Deeply moved, I read what was over this arch, spelled out for all time in metallic letters:

I.K. BRUNEL
Engineer 1859

I pulled up the window and settled back in my seat. Holmes was again deep in the study of his maps. I now preferred to enjoy the scenery passing before the window, which changed again as we drew further inland. Shortly after half past four, we arrived at Bodmin Road station, where we left the train, claimed our luggage, and, to our great pleasure, were already awaited by Silvanus Jenkins, Lord Robartes' steward.

Lanhydrock

Holmes and I took our places in the rear of the covered carriage, which his lordship had provided for our arrival. As soon as the luggage had been transferred, and Mr. Jenkins had taken his place opposite us in the carriage, the coachman set the horses in motion. Shortly we left the Bodmin Road and turned off into a delightful avenue of trees. Mr. Jenkins explained that this avenue had been planted especially to assure an agreeable journey between Lanhydrock and the station. From the window I fancied I saw red deer on both sides of the avenue. I mentioned this to Mr. Jenkins, who assured me that red deer had been settled in the park for at least a hundred years. As I looked in the hope of seeing more, an impressive gatehouse came into sight, and we drew up towards it. I saw then that the gatehouse was set in a low battlemented wall, enclosing the garden of Lanhydrock House.

"We seem to have arrived", I said, turning to Holmes; He however only nodded, and continued to study the scene. "Quite so, Dr. Watson", was Mr. Jenkins' friendly comment.

Since Holmes was clearly not ready to talk with me, I addressed my next observation to the steward. "With the two massive towers, each side of the gate and the battlements on top, this gatehouse is truly impressive."

"It is indeed a most distinctive gatehouse, Dr. Watson, dating from the 17th century, and was originally a hunting lodge. From the upstairs windows one could watch the hunt and perhaps even see the kill. In this century it was at first a porter's lodge, and for the last ten years the Sunday School for the surrounding district has used the upstairs rooms".

"Mr. Jenkins, you are well-informed over Lanhydrock and its background," I remarked appreciatively. "Thank you for that friendly word, Dr. Watson. It is true; Lanhydrock lies close to my heart. I grew up here, and have learned about the house from my father, just as he learned about it from his father, and each one from his father before him. Our family has had the privilege of serving the house of Robartes-Agar for more than a hundred years."

The deep attachment to Lanhydrock and its owners, which so clearly motivated these words of Mr. Jenkins, had moved me, and I could now understand better the affection in his expression, as he looked out upon all around him. Following his attention, I now saw before us a great three-storey granite building. It was built to a U-shaped ground plan, with the open side towards us. Lanhydrock House consists of a long central part in the west, with two adjoining wings on the north and south ends. On the south side there are several other buildings, stables and a carriage shed. On both sides of the gravel drive, there are extensive gardens, and beyond the north wing I saw a geometrically laid out garden, separated by hedges. Despite the advancing season, this was full with various richly blooming flowers. For a moment, I had to think how my dear Mary's heart would have rejoiced to see such a display. But the call of our coachman to halt, and a sudden silence of the wheels on the gravel, broke into my thoughts.

Hardly had Holmes and I descended from the carriage than we were surrounded by barking and a deep growling. Two powerful Labradors, the one white, the other black, were watching us suspiciously, and were only calmed when Mr. Jenkins took them by the collars and spoke a quiet order. "Unusual," murmured Mr. Jenkins. Then he turned to us: "Please forgive this somewhat aggressive reception, Mr. Holmes, Dr. Watson. Someone has let the dogs off their chains. That is really most unusual." Shaking his head and obviously puzzled, he gave the dogs to the coachman, who was trying to calm the horses, made restive by the dogs' behaviour. "George, take Snowy and Sooty to the stable and send us two stable boys, to look after the luggage of these gentlemen."

"Yes, Mr Jenkins", replied the coachman and disappeared at once with the two dogs, trotting obediently alongside him, through the nearby arch.

While the stable boys unloaded our luggage, we entered the house through a double door. Mr. Jenkins led the way, so I had no opportunity to study the inner door, which was in oak and carried an elaborate coat of arms. It was clear that Mr. Jenkins was somewhat disturbed; he asked us now to wait, and disappeared through a swing-door at the end of the hall. As we waited, my eyes wandered over the hall and its low, geometric patterned ceiling, the stucco relief, and the oak panelling, and finally the great fireplace in granite, which dominated the back wall with its size and form. I turned to the window just as Mr. Jenkins appeared again and, with some embarrassment, said: "I must apologise in the name of his Lordship, for this less than adequate reception. There has apparently been during my absence a small mishap, which has somewhat distracted the household. The butler and housekeeper should have received you and shown you to your rooms. This duty now falls to me. Would you please kindly follow me?" He turned again through the swing door, and Holmes and I followed.

An impressive oaken staircase rose before us. On our left was a further large room, the inner hall. A further staircase in teak appeared at the far end of this room. Mr. Jenkins explained that both staircases led to the private rooms of his Lordship's family, on the first floor, and that these were only used by the family of his Lordship, and their guests. As we climbed the stairs, Mr. Jenkins explained that in the whole house a clear separation by gender and by social status was maintained, as indeed is recommended by Mr Robert Kerr, in his useful book "A Gentleman's House." Coming to the first floor, we followed the corridor before us, passing the teak staircase, and then turned right to a corridor leading to the south wing. All at once I discovered on a chest a large model of a rowing boat. Mr. Jenkins, although leading, noticed at once my interest and stopped. I studied the model carefully as he explained:

"In 1863 the first Lord Robartes gave to the coastal region of The Lizard a lifeboat. The people of the district were poor, and were most grateful for this gesture, because such a boat cost even then some two hundred pounds. They could never have paid for it themselves. In gratitude they named the lifeboat Agar-Robartes, and some years later His Lordship received this model."

While I thanked Mr. Jenkins for this information, and as I was ready to go on, Holmes suddenly spoke. "Mr. Jenkins, you spoke earlier of a small mishap, which had occurred during your absence. May I ask what has happened?"

"But naturally, Mr. Holmes. Shortly after I left Lanhydrock, a fire broke out in a stable building. It was quickly discovered, and could fortunately be quickly extinguished by the staff. But fear of fire is something we all have in Lanhydrock. The destructive fire of ten years ago not only destroyed the south, and part of the west, wing, but has left all who live here with some deep, although invisible, scars. That is also why his Lordship had a large water reservoir built, in the upper gardens behind the west wing. Moreover, for the rebuilding of Lanhydrock his Lordship also insisted that all ceilings should no longer be of wooden beams, but executed in solid, fifteen inch thick reinforced concrete." Holmes appeared satisfied with this answer, and we continued along the corridor before us, without further comment.

At the end were our guest rooms, and there was another staircase, which, Mr. Jenkins said, was only used by the female house staff. I had been given the corner bedroom with alcove, in an extension of the south wing, while Holmes had the eastern bedroom, in the end of the south wing. Before we took up our rooms, Mr. Jenkins confirmed that our luggage had been placed in the correct dressing rooms, and that our washing jugs had been filled with hot water. Obviously satisfied with what he found, he gave a smile of some relief, and turned to us again: "Dinner will be served at seven o'clock. His Lordship will await you in the Inner Hall. You have now time to refresh yourselves, and to dress for dinner. If you have no further wishes, I would now leave you."

"Thank you, Mr. Jenkins. You may go", replied Holmes, as did I. With a courteous bow, Mr. Jenkins turned on his heel and walked briskly back along the corridor by which we had come, leaving us to prepare for dinner.

As I descended to enter the Inner Hall with Holmes, there awaited already a lady and gentleman dressed for dinner, and my expectation that these were our hosts was quickly confirmed. "Mr. Holmes, Dr. Watson, also on behalf of my dear wife, I would like to welcome you most warmly to Lanhydrock. I was very pleased that you chose to undertake the long journey, so as to devote your attention to the matters which, in recent times, have caused me care and anxiety. But we will speak later of this. Let us first enjoy the pleasures, in which we will all participate, of dinner in good company." Holmes nodded courteously at the words of Lord Robartes, and I was about to thank him for my part, when I was interrupted by the arrival of two more gentlemen in dinner dress. They were clearly good friends of the Robartes family, and were introduced as the Reverend Hubert Carlyon, and Mr. Tremayne. It was apparent that both were regular readers of the "Strand' Magazine," in which I had had published some accounts of various adventures of my friend Sherlock Holmes. Both seemed agreeably surprised to see for themselves that the great detective from London's Baker Street was not in fact merely a literary figure. The guests being now all-present, Lord Robartes offered his Lady his arm, in an unmistakeable sign that we should follow him into the dining room.

When, after dinner, coffee was served, there developed a discussion led chiefly by the Rev. Carlyon. He had, by his description, been for the last two years vicar of the Parish of St. Just in Roseland. St. Just, on the Roseland peninsular, lies, as I understood him, some twenty-seven miles southwest of Lanhydrock. An agreeable person, he was full of praise for his church, which dates from the 13th century, and for his parishioners, with whom he had established a wide contact. Apart from his calling to the service of God, he seemed to have one further enthusiasm, namely, beekeeping. He was full of praise for the new beehives which Mr. Tremayne had installed at his country seat at Heligan. Mr. Tremayne was obviously touched by the praise of Rev. Carlyon, and so started to tell us more about Heligan, his house and its gardens. The estate appears to date from the 12th century, but came first in the Tudor period into the Tremayne family. A hundred years ago, his predecessor Henry Hawkins Tremayne began to lay out an extraordinary garden. "Every generation which came after him has since then pursued this passion, and that includes myself," said Mr. Tremayne with a smile and continued: "There are at present twenty-two gardeners in my service. It is thanks to their skill that, among other things, the rhododendron seeds which a plant collector recently brought to this country from the Himalayas, and the tree ferns from New Zealand, have slowly become established."

These observations led Lord Robartes to start an animated discussion with Mr. Tremayne about this year's harvest. I thought that botany and agriculture might now dominate the table round, but I was wrong. Holmes, who had remained withdrawn during this conversation, suddenly addressed himself with interest to the Reverend Carlyon. "Beekeeping appeals to me as an occupation which I might well pursue, when my days as a consulting detective are past. The prospect of retirement to Sussex, to study the industrious habits of these community-building creatures, holds much attraction for me." I looked across in surprise at my friend, but before I could speak, he and the Reverend were already deep in conversation about beekeeping. I heard Mr. Carlyon say: "Mr. Holmes, before you make any start with beekeeping, I recommend that you read the monograph 'Bees, Their Habits and Management,' by the naturalist J.G. Wood. Although this work was written twenty-five years ago, it still rates as required reading for would-be beekeepers."

Since my interest in bees extended only to the proper treatment of bee-stings, and my knowledge of plants embraced primarily their value for herbal remedies, I was no natural conversational partner for the gentlemen. Perhaps I might be better advised to address myself to Lady Robartes, sitting on my right towards the head of the table. I determined to ask her about the central table decoration, a great silver ornament, which stood before us. It was of an elaborate and exotic form, eye-catching and dignified, representing an oasis scene with a high-standing palm tree, with at the base a crystal bowl full of fruit. "Lady Robartes, I have been greatly admiring this table piece." A warm and friendly smile came to her lips as she replied: "Thank you, Dr. Watson, yes, it is truly most decorative, and is unique in its form. For my husband and me, however, it is the ideal which it represents which makes it important to us." My look expressed my curiosity, and she continued: "This table piece was presented in 1869 to my husband's father, by the mine workers of Redruth. The base of the work is not, as one might expect, of silver, but of Cornish tin. The miners wanted to show in this way their gratitude for the support which Lord and Lady Robartes had given to the establishment of a miners' hospital."

She had with these words commanded my interest, but before I could say more, she turned and quietly said: "But now I would like to return to my rooms, and rest quietly. The excitement of this afternoon seems to have demanded its tribute from me." She smiled and rose; and we did likewise. "If the gentlemen would kindly excuse me, I will now withdraw. I wish you an agreeable evening and a good night." The butler had already drawn back her chair, so that she could leave the table. She was not quite at the door, leading to the inner hall, as Lord Robartes approached and stood beside her. Gently he took her hand, kissed it, and watched affectionately as she withdrew. He then turned to us and said: "The gentlemen will surely agree that the time has come to take an excellent whisky and address the problem we have before us. May I invite you to accompany me to the smoking room?"

The Problem

When we had all found our places in the smoking room, and had been provided with tobacco and whisky, Lord Robartes spoke to us all. "Gentlemen, I hope you have found the evening just as interesting and stimulating as I have. Regrettably, the reason why we meet here at Lanhydrock is not one which is designed to please us. In recent times curious things have been occurring, which have also involved Mr Tremayne and Rev. Carlyon. I therefore hope that Mr. Holmes will soon be able, either to reassure me, or to cast light upon these events."

Lord Robartes, as he said this, looked expectantly at Holmes. There was a short pause, before my friend replied: "It will surely be best, Lord Robartes, if you simply describe to me what is troubling you. Please be sure to omit no details, even if they appear unimportant." Hardly had my friend said this then he leaned back, closed his eyes and laid his fingertips together. The casual observer might have thought he was sleeping, and indeed, Lord Robartes appeared at first irritated, as if that were what he was thinking. As I brought out my notebook, however, and prepared to make my notes, Lord Robartes had already overcome his surprise, and spoke with a firm voice of his experience. "Together with Lady Robartes and the children, I always spend the summer in London. In my absence, Lanhydrock House, and the surrounding lands, are managed by my steward, Mr. Jenkins. Should anything untoward arise, he makes contact with me by telegraph. So it was in August of this year. There was an enquiry from a lawyer's practice in Fowey, concerning a former house servant and her service here. I gave him permission to assist the lawyer, and so Mr. Jenkins received, a few days later, a Mr. Ian Reeve, whose visit had been advised in advance by the lawyer's office."

At this point the energetic voice of my friend broke into Lord Robartes' account.

"It would be preferable if Mr. Jenkins could himself describe this visit."

Disturbed at first, Lord Robartes accorded my friend his wish, and since Mr. Jenkins was in his nearby office and occupied by entries in the estate books, he appeared quickly at the door of the smoking room. He looked with some surprise at those seated before him, until Lord Robartes addressed him: "Mr. Jenkins, would you kindly describe to us the visit of Mr Ian Reeves from the Fowey lawyer's practice? Please leave nothing out, however unimportant it may seem."

Holmes nodded to Lord Robartes his agreement, and I felt a certain amusement, caused by Lord Robartes' anxiety to meet Holmes' instruction not to omit details. Mr. Jenkins coughed, and then with clear voice presented his report.

"Mr. Hoole, the lawyer of Fowey, had written to His Lordship at Lanhydrock House in the second week in August, to seek information concerning a former female servant at Lanhydrock. His Lordship was at this time in London, so I telegraphed to ask his permission. On receiving this, I replied positively, to the lawyer, who in return announced to me the visit of his clerk, Mr. Ian Reeve. When he came, I was at first concerned, as his appearance was somewhat neglected. He was however most courteous and correct, and his manner was certainly better than his appearance. I showed him the servants' register, from which he took the information he required in his notebook. Clearly satisfied with my help, and with what he had found, he took his leave, but with the request that I might in the following days take the register to the practice, so that Mr. Hoole, the lawyer, could see it himself. I did this, and so there is really no more to report."

Mr. Jenkins looked at Lord Robartes, but Holmes at once broke in with a question. "Mr. Jenkins, do you recall the name of the servant, in which the lawyer's practice was interested?"

"Yes, Mr. Holmes, I do. The name was Ruth Oakley. As I recall, she had come to Lanhydrock House in the spring of 1853. She came from the orphanage in Bodmin and was thirteen years old, when she came to the House. I should explain that a house such as Lanhydrock requires a staff of around eighty persons. Most are taken from the surrounding region, and whenever possible we take some from the orphanage. The married staff live in the vicinity, but those that are single, including naturally those from the orphanage, live in Lanhydrock House. Ruth Oakley appears to have had an aptitude for learning, as she began work in the scullery, but by the time she left she had already become a lady's maid to the later Lady Robartes. She left on grounds of her forthcoming marriage to Mr. David Lang. He was the second youngest son in the building firm of Thomas Lang & Sons, of Liskeard. I suspect that she met that young man during work being undertaken here in 1864." Mr. Jenkins looked again first at Lord Robartes, and then at Holmes, who opened his eyes and said: "Thank you, Mr. Jenkins."

Since my friend was obviously satisfied with Mr. Jenkins' account, Lord Robartes dismissed the steward with "Thank you, Mr. Jenkins; you may go." Satisfied that he was free to leave the smoking room, Mr. Jenkins bowed politely to Lord Robartes and left us to continue.

Lord Robartes now asked Rev. Carlyon to present his contribution to the problem. I had for my part to admit that I had not seen anything that suggested a problem to me. Perhaps however there was more to come, which the vicar's words might reveal.

"On the 19th August I also had a visit from Mr. Ian Reeve. He came with an introductory letter, from the lawyer's practice of Mr. Hoole in Fowey. This reassured me somewhat, for, as Mr. Jenkins has said, his appearance was somewhat neglected, and it was not enhanced by his striking red hair. He told me that his task was to find a certain Ruth Oakley, as Mr. Hoole had in his care a legacy, which, when all was proved correct, was to be given to her. Mr. Reeve told me that he had learned that she had married, and that her husband was Mr. David Lang, a son of the Lang family, builders in Liskeard. His enquiries had revealed that shortly after the marriage, Mr David Lang and his wife had moved to St. Just in Roseland, to build up his own business. Mr.

Reeve asked me whether the couple still lived in St. Just. I could readily confirm this; they are known, loved and respected far beyond my parish. Mr Lang had only last autumn renovated the church roof, charging only for his materials and offering his work free. Mrs. Lang is always ready to help where there is need, and most friendly. There are sadly no children, but she is a second mother to the apprentice in their workshop. These are two admirable people. Indeed, they remind me of another most agreeable and elderly couple in my former parish, who are now regrettably dead, but..." The good clergyman was however interrupted in his discourse over bygone days, as Lord Robartes gently suggested: "My dear friend, I think it will be more helpful to Mr. Holmes, if you could tell us of your experience in Fowey."

"Naturally; forgive me. I fear that in good company I am sometimes tempted to wander from the subject", he replied, with some embarrassment, and then continued:

"Mr. Reeve decided to visit Mrs. Lang, if possible on the same day. He asked me to accompany him. I did so gladly, and so I was there, when he told the good lady that there was a bequest waiting for her in Fowey. Mrs. Lang could scarcely believe that anyone could have left anything to her, for, as she repeatedly said, except for her husband and his brothers she had no other relatives. She could barely recall her father and her older brother, Silas, for they had both, as her mother had explained to her, one day failed to return from fishing out at sea. Like most fishing families, they were very poor, and so they soon found themselves in the workhouse. This was more an existence than a life, in that dreadful place of hopelessness, and then Ruth's mother fell ill with typhus fever, and soon died. Thanks to the clergyman who conducted the pauper's funeral, Ruth was taken away to the orphanage in Bodmin. There, four years went by, until Lady Juliana Robartes brought her to Lanhydrock, where she had for the first time a sense of having found somewhere to call home. I had been very moved by this account of Mrs Lang's young life, and so I scarcely heard Mr Reeve as he said that she would soon have an invitation to the lawyer's chambers, in Fowey. He then took his leave of us, but I remained a little longer with Mrs. Lang, until she had somewhat recovered."

The Rev. Carlyon paused here, sipped his whisky and then continued his account. "Three days later I went with her, as she had earnestly requested me to do, to the lawyer's chambers in Fowey. The lawyer, Mr. Hoole, was most friendly and accommodating. As soon as Mr Reeve and I had given our solemn assurance that we indeed could identify Mrs. Lang, she was given a casket with a key. That good lady at first was most reluctant to open the casket, but finally overcame her fear and allowed her curiosity to lead her. The casket was stuffed full of small, unpromising leather purses. She timidly took one out and opened it, to shake something of the contents onto her hand. Puzzled, and nervous, she looked at her hand and then at me. Before I could do more, however, Mr. Reeve broke out with a quivering voice: "My goodness! That is gold. The casket contains a fortune."

The lawyer disapproved sharply of this indiscretion by his clerk, who immediately fell quiet. Mrs Lang, understandably, fainted, and I was concerned, how I might bring her safely back to St. Just. She recovered, however, with the help of smelling salts, and her first question was, from whom the lawyer had received the casket. He however insisted that he must respect the anonymity of his client, on which the latter had explicitly insisted. I observed that for Mrs. Lang, the situation was at present too much to judge clearly. I proposed that she should return to St. Just, to sleep on the matter. I advised that she take the key with her, but that the casket should remain in the care of the lawyer, in his safe. We would then return home by the quickest way, and then discuss the matter with her husband. Mrs. Lang agreed, and so we prepared to leave. She was still understandably weak from the shock, so that I was grateful that Mr. Reeve helped me to bring her below to the street. Before we were on the pavement, I caught something, as he muttered a few words to Mrs. Lang. To my surprise, he had obviously offered to betray the name of her benefactor, if she would pay him. Mrs. Lang took her small purse, and shook the modest contents into the greedy hand extended to her. He saw that the few coins were of no great value, and muttered bitterly: "What does it matter? His name is Simon Osborn". Then he turned on his heel, and disappeared.

"Perhaps I should have intervened, but my concern was for Mrs. Lang, still shocked, who could only mutter that she knew of no Simon Osborn. The journey back to St. Just taxed us both, and I assure you that a stone fell from my heart as I finally gave her into the care of her husband. In the meantime she had recovered from her shock. Together with her husband they have recovered the casket from the lawyer's office and deposited it at the bank. They are both full of plans, to make the best use of the money. They think to enlarge the workshop and employ two more apprentices.

Their house needs a new roof, and the church in St. Just also requires repairs. For my part I have to decide what is more important, new hymn books or the restoration of an old window. Or perhaps I should first...." He came no further, however, as Lord Robartes interrupted him again. "My dear friend, thank you for your account. It think it is now time to hear what Mr Tremayne has to report."

I had up to this point not yet been able to recognise what might be the problem that Holmes and I were called to solve. Unusual it may have been, but with the best will I could not see in all this a threat or danger. I could not linger on this thought because Mr Tremayne now, without hesitation, began his account. "On September 11 I was at Mevagissey Harbour, where I was expecting a delivery of some exotic plants, and I wanted to see them delivered safely and undamaged to Heligan. I was watching as the incoming vessel laid alongside, and a few paces away another vessel was being worked. Suddenly, while I was watching my ship, perhaps through a careless moment, a great barrel slipped, fell and burst with a loud report, almost at my feet. I must admit that for a moment my heart seemed at the shock to stand still. Most relieved to have escaped the danger, I only at a second look noticed what was pouring out of the barrel at my feet." At this point Mr. Tremayne paused briefly, took a deep draft of his whisky, and then continued in a solemn voice. "Surrounded by swarms of pilchards, all laid in salt, was the body of a dead man." Appalled, I looked at Mr. Tremayne, who now was refilling his whisky glass. It was clear that he was, as he told his story, reliving this gruesome moment, and sought now desperately to recover his normal demeanour. I was relieved, when he was after a few moments able to continue.

"The dead man was a stranger to me, and yet I had a feeling that I had seen him before. His fiery red hair, through which ran bands of grey, had somewhere come to my attention and remained in my memory. But in that environment, and with the fright I had sustained, I could not bring the concentration to say where I might have seen him. A day or so later, however I saw in the newspaper that he had recently been employed in the practice of Mr. Hoole, the lawyer in Fowey. His name was Ian Reeve and he had obvious substantial gambling debts, so that the police were led to think he may have been murdered for his debts. I had barely read the article, when I remembered where I had last seen Mr Reeve; it was on the 5th September, a Friday, as I was in St. Austell to order a barrel of beer. Close to the brewery is a house of doubtful repute, in which is located the Fortuna Club.

The members of this club can play cards in the lower rooms, while on the upper floor, please excuse me, mmm, how should I say, a rather more questionable establishment seems to be able, despite the law, to offer its services. Whatever this may tell us, it was there that I saw this person, then quite unknown, and whom I now know as Mr Reeve, coming out. Despite his striking hair, I might have forgotten him at once, had he not been in the company of Mr. Willoughby Pascoe, as he left that establishment. Mr Pascoe has, since an unpleasant business matter, left me with a most disagreeable feeling for him. The two appeared together. They seemed to know one another well, and to be on most friendly terms. That seemed to me remarkable enough, for old Mr Pascoe is everywhere here well-known for his rudeness and hard-hearted attitude. With the young Mr. Reeve, however, he had laid his arm around Reeve's shoulder in an almost fatherly manner. Be that as it may, at the weekend I told Rev. Carlyon, to whom I had paid a friendly visit in St. Just, of my frightful experience in Mevagissey, and that I had seen the dead man with Mr. Pascoe, and Reverend Carlyon told me with surprise that he too had make the acquaintance of Mr. Reeve." With this, Mr. Tremayne completed his account, and looked across to Lord Robartes.

His Lordship nodded briefly and spoke to us himself. "Thank you, Mr Tremayne, for these observations. Now it is my turn, Mr. Holmes, and Dr. Watson, to tell you what I know. I too have met Mr. Reeve once, although I did not know him. This was on August 27th as I visited Mr. Reginald Dunston in St. Austell. Mr. Reeve gave me the impression that he was hanging about in the street, and observing the house of Mr. Dunston. I too noted his fiercely red hair. I even suspected that he might be a burglar preparing to break in on Mr. Dunston, who was in poor health. I determined to challenge him, but at that moment he turned about and walked away, to disappear into the White Hart Hotel. I was not going to follow him, but decided it would be better to tell Mr. Dunston what I had observed, and to recommend that he take precautions. This I did, and I might have thought no more about it, had I not, as did Mr. Tremayne, retained a recollection of Mr. Reeve's red hair. When therefore a few days ago Mr. Tremayne told me of his experiences in Mevagissey at the harbour, and of his conversation with Rev. Carlyon, I also realised that I had seen the dead man.

This may now all strike you as coincidence, but two other circumstances may help to show these events in a different light. For this, however, I will tell you a little of the background. As you may now know, Lanhydrock House was the casualty, almost ten years ago, of a devastating fire. After the fire we resolved to rebuild it as it had been, but with some alterations. One of the changes which we made concerned the laundry. There had been a wash-house and laundry at Lanhydrock, but we found it appropriate that this work should now be entrusted to a charitable foundation. Various neighbours joined us in this project, and in the meantime therefore, the 'House of Merry' in Bodmin and the 'St. Faith Home for Fallen Women' in Lostwithiel have become established institutions. We intend to establish one in St. Austell and I am ready to donate the land, as I did in Lostwithiel. The land I had in view had belonged originally to Mr. Pascoe, but I bought it from him last year. Since he had, unusually, not demanded an exaggerated price, and as during the building work we would need to cross a patch of land still in his possession, it seemed wise to retain his good will. I invited him therefore with other benefactors to the formal occasion of a foundation stone laying. One of the benefactors is Mr. Dunstan, but he had declined my written invitation. I had visited him personally, in the hope of persuading him, and that was just on the day when I saw Mr. Reeve. Although Mr. Dunstan seemed genuinely touched by my concern, when I came to leave him he had still not given his word. Perhaps he changed his mind, but that the world will now never know."

Lord Robartes interrupted his account to take a draft of his whisky, as had earlier Mr. Tremayne, before he could continue with a more subdued voice. "His housekeeper found him dead in his library, on the morning of September 15th. That good lady had spent the weekend with her sister, and came back to St. Austell on Monday morning. It was well known that Mr Dunston's health was not of the best, but his death nevertheless caused some concern in the region. Indeed, I reflected, whether it might not be better, so close to my celebration, to postpone the ceremony. However, William Gladstone, the former Prime Minister, who will be the patron of the Foundation Charity, has already accepted my invitation as guest of honour, and could scarcely offer an alternative date at short notice. Winter is approaching, and a delay would surely mean that building would only start next year. Since I did not feel ready to decide alone, I telegraphed all the sponsors, and Mr. Pascoe, from whom I had bought the land, to ask their opinion. Except for Mr. Pascoe, all replied asking me to uphold the agreed date. I resolved to visit Mr. Pascoe, but when I called in Lostwithiel at his home, I learned from his housekeeper that he had already been away some days. Mr. Pascoe is certainly not an easy person; and I felt that his housekeeper might even have been relieved when he was away. She told me, however, that he was often away for several days, giving neither an indication of his destination, nor of the length of his absence. As she told me that Mr Pascoe had come home on the afternoon of September 5th from his occupations in St. Austell, and had packed his toilet needs, his slippers, and fresh linen, in his small travelling bag, and had again left the house, I had nevertheless a troubled sensation. That was just the day on which Mr. Tremayne had observed him leaving the Fortuna Club."

Lord Robartes paused again, before continuing, this time more decisively, to say: "Mr. Holmes, everything that you have heard this evening may be no more than a series of unrelated events, the result of a series of coincidences. Those authorities who are here responsible for the maintenance of good order, took exactly that view as I visited the police station in Bodmin. I cannot however exclude, that there is perhaps more in these events than first appears. You must also consider, Mr. Holmes, that here in Cornwall we are in the midst of an election campaign. There have already been some ugly scenes, and I am most concerned to avoid any unpleasantness at my forthcoming foundation-stone laying. And apart from this, I must be sure that none of us is in any kind of danger. That is especially so for those I count among my friends".

After these words, an uncomfortable silence hung in the smoking room. All eyes were on Holmes, who sat as before, with eyes closed, in his armchair. He slowly opened his eyes and looked searchingly at Lord Robartes. "Sir, those occurrences which you and your friends have reported may indeed, when we regard each one individually, not appear of any importance. Considered together, however, there may well be more in these circumstances than may at first appear. First, however, a question: Who are the benefactors of your forthcoming house in St. Austell?"

"First comes our former Prime Minister, William Ewart Gladstone, and then the Rev. Carlyon, Mr. Tremayne, the late Mr. Dunstan, and finally indirectly, Mr. Pascoe, who sold me the land. And I also have donated."

"Thank you, Lord Robartes", acknowledged Holmes, who then continued, after a further short pause, and without visible emotion:

"It would please me to occupy myself with this matter on your behalf."

"Mr. Holmes, I am most grateful to you", said Lord Robartes. His obvious relief that the whole matter now rested in Holmes' competent hands, was readily apparent. Rev. Carlyon and Mr. Tremayne also showed their satisfaction. The tension began to lessen, and as Lord Robartes proposed a short game in the billiards room, as relaxation, all accepted his proposal. My friend, however, excused himself and chose to remain in the smoking room with his thoughts, in front of the warm hearth.

I found that the billiards room adjoined the smoking room directly. It was occupied by a large and fine billiard table in mahogany, and a richly ornamented chimney, with a mantelpiece on which were a number of prize cups. Reading the engraving, one in particular caught my attention. I heard Lord Robartes voice behind me: "My father was a great cricket lover, and was indeed the first Cornish member of the Marylebone Cricket Club. My interest lay with billiards. Even as a student, in Oxford, at Christ Church College, I passed much of my free time in the billiard halls of the town. But come, Dr. Watson, the other two gentlemen have already taken up cue and chalk." The game helped each of us to relax, and it was clear that Lord Robartes not only loved this sport, but had also mastered it to perfection. My game went gradually from indifferent to worse, which I could fortunately attribute both to the late hour and to the long train journey. It was clearly time that I withdrew to go to bed. Apologising to my fellow players, I looked into the smoking room, but Holmes' armchair was now empty. I thus withdrew, half asleep already, to find my bedroom, in by the sincere hope that I could find my way in this warren of passages and staircases.

The list

On waking next morning, I resolved to make, at the first opportunity, a sketch-map of the district. The place names which I had heard last night were all unknown to me, and revolved in confusion in my head. When I would find time would depend, of course, on the plans which Holmes might have for the day. I knocked gently on his door, but when there was no reply I assumed he must already be at breakfast, and went down to the lower hall, where I found Lord Robartes, the Rev. Carlyon und Mr. Tremayne engaged in an energetic conversation. As I entered, they accorded me a brief smile and friendly "Good morning," but there was clearly a tension in the air. I had to ask: "Lord Robartes, has something happened?"

"Yes, Dr. Watson. One of the kitchen maids found this note this morning, close to where yesterday the fire had so alarmed us." With these words he passed me a sheet of writing paper, on which stood the following:

YOUR LIBERAL ATTITUDE IS A DISGRACE TO YOUR RANK

NO FURTHER HELP FOR THE LIBERAL PARTY FIRE IS OFTEN THE ONLY WAY TO PURGE EVIL AND TO OVERCOME FALSE BELIEFS

Shocked, I read these few lines and at once said: "This is a disgraceful threat, Lord Robartes! Have you already shown it to Sherlock Holmes?"

"Regrettably not, Dr. Watson. Mr. Holmes left the house very early this morning."

I looked in surprise at Lord Robartes, who explained: "Jenkins brought Mr. Holmes to the station at dawn. It seems he had asked Jenkins yesterday evening, and explained his intention. As I have instructed Jenkins to fulfil wherever possible the wishes both of Mr. Holmes and naturally of yourself, Dr. Watson, he brought Mr. Holmes in the carriage to the station, and will meet him again there this evening. Mr. Holmes told him that he expected to have a first round of enquiries completed by then, and that he would be punctually back for dinner." Troubled, and somewhat irritated that Holmes had begun his investigations without me, I went with the others to breakfast.

After breakfast Mr. Tremayne and the Rev. Carlyon took their leave of me, as the time was come for them to travel home. Lord Robartes had offered to accompany them to the station, as he intended to go to the Bodmin Police Station with the threatening letter. I was therefore alone, and given the beautiful weather that morning, I resolved to go out. I told Mr. Jenkins that I would be pleased to go fishing, whereupon, to my delight, he told me that there was a small lake, well stocked, not far from Lanhydrock House. It was thus that, not much later, I was sitting with my rod and basket on the bank of a truly serene pool. As I had determined not to break off for lunch at the house, Mr. Jenkins had instructed the kitchen to prepare me a small picnic. The opportunity was therefore perfect, together with my provisions, to enjoy the calm and quiet here by the water. I caught nothing, but my annoyance and disappointment over Holmes' disappearance had at least subsided. What remained was the thankfulness, in this threatening situation, that I had been able to spend a most agreeable and recreational day in the country.

Back at Lanhydrock House I resolved, as I had earlier determined, to sketch out my plan of the district. I required first of all a large-scale topographical map, for which I first asked Mr. Jenkins. He led me to the great library, which contained a collection of works on the most varied subjects. In particular he showed me the almost two hundred year old Lanhydrock Atlas, which was, he said, still in use, and which had newly been re-bound in leather. This Atlas is in four volumes, and contains two-hundred-and-fifty-eight superb watercolours on parchment, each page being some sixteen by twenty inches. The colourful maps are not signed, but are attributed to Joel Gascogne, who may, dear reader, be known to some. In the seventeenth century he was one of the leading cartographers of his time. A particular speciality of the Lanhydrock Atlas is that not only the properties and boundaries, but also houses, streets, tenancies and tenants are all shown in great detail. Even the use of the land, for forest, meadows, grazing and parkland is to be found. The reader will not therefore be surprised to learn that in the library I found no problem in making a simple, clear sketch plan of the main features and places of the district. I put it safely in my notebook to add to it during our stay as necessary. In writing of this adventure subsequently, I resolved, for the interested reader, to include this map with my account.

The Library contained so many literary treasures that it gave great pleasure just to walk along the bookcases, to study the spines and titles of the books, and to take out an occasional work. So I found "Antiquities," historical and monumental, of the Country of Cornwall', with many engravings of objects which were to me completely unknown. I suddenly became aware that Lord Robartes was beside me. He looked with interest at the book in my hands and said: "This is the second, enlarged edition of the work of the Reverend William Borlase, the vicar of Penwith. It appeared in 1769, fifteen years after the first edition. When you would learn more on the history of Cornwall, I can recommend most warmly all his books, Dr. Watson. You will find them here in this library." I was indeed interested, but had to say: "The author is completely unknown to me, but the engravings in the book already fascinated me."

Obviously pleased at my interest, Lord Robartes continued: "William Borlase was from a long-established Cornish family, whose pedigree went back to William the Conqueror. He studied at Exeter College in Oxford, and was later ordained. He was however not only a man of God, but a most committed researcher in antiquities and natural history. In his first edition he noted that he had studied the antiquities of his own countrymen, because he could not visit Greece. It is to this that we can gratefully attribute his keenly detailed documentation of our own early past. The engravings which have interested you, Dr. Watson, were all made by William Borlase by his own hand. The clarity and precision of this work shows that he had doubtless a most developed talent."

During Lord Robartes' words, I had nodded in agreement, and looked even more respectfully at a page that I had just found. It showed several views of an object, like a small house, made out of seven great stones, one in front, two at the sides, and a fallen rear wall, and over the whole a twelve feet long sloping roof stone. This had a hole in one corner. It appeared that these stones enclosed a chamber of about six feet long and, at their highest point, a height of some twelve feet. But who could have built such a structure, and to what purpose? Clearly it was very old, and I found myself wondering how those who built it could have done so. Lord Robartes followed my expression, for he explained: "This print shows Trethevy Quoit, which some call the Giant's House. You will come upon this stone edifice if you take the road from Liskeard towards the Cheesewring and The Hurlers."

Mystified, I looked at Lord Robartes, and he gave me, somewhat amused, another explanation. "When you take the road from Liskeard to the village of Minions, you will reach the southern edge of Bodmin Moor. To the east are the abandoned workings of the great Caradon mines. To the west is a hill, on the summit of which is a curious structure of granite platforms. The whole appears like a collection of great cheeses, piled on one another, and this is surely the explanation of the name, the Cheesewring. Remarkable is that the highest stones are the biggest, so that the whole appears quite top-heavy. Whether this too is a relic of long-lost cultures, or simply a trick of nature, no-one knows. There are however many legends which are associated with the district." As he spoke, Lord Robartes took the book carefully from my hand, to seek another print. "And these are The Hurlers," he said, as he gave me back the book."

"Why they have this name, I will explain directly. They need however first some explanation. The whole structure is clearly the work of human hands. It consists of three circles of great stones, the middle one being the biggest, with diameter of about a hundred and thirty-six feet. As the print here shows, the southern circle is the least well preserved. Only two stones remain standing, the others now lying, and sometimes buried. This upright stone, standing alone, is known as the Piper." Lord Robartes noted my surprise and continued his account with some amusement. "That brings us to the name of the site, which stems from another legend. This recounts that on a religious feast day, a number of men and women had preferred to play their country game of hurling, using wooden clubs and a leather ball. They were entertained during the game by a piper. The moral of the tale comes, however, that they were all turned to stone, for hurling when they should have been in church." Before I could respond, however, Lord Robartes reminded me gently, that time was advancing: "I think we have had enough of legend and history for today, Dr. Watson. We have now to think of dinner." I was surprised, on consulting my watch, to realise that it was already half past six. How quickly the time had slipped away in this glorious library! I thanked Lord Robartes for his kindness, and returned to my room to dress for dinner.

As I then returned to the inner hall, I found Lord and Lady Robartes in conversation with Holmes. Whatever he had been doing, he had returned as promised to dinner. Only too gladly would I have spoken with him about his plans when he went off alone, but before I could say anything, Lord Robartes intervened: "I hope, Dr. Watson, that you have spent an agreeable day. Mr. Holmes was obviously very busy and has certainly matters on which he can report. That can however wait until after dinner." With this, he smiled to his Lady and led her into the dining room, while Holmes and I followed silently. As we settled again in the smoking room as on the previous evening, Lord Robartes first described the finding of the threatening letter. Holmes, who had been up to this point quiet, was at once interested. Turning to his Lordship, he said: "Please describe, exactly, how this letter came into your possession"

"One of the kitchen maids found it, by the door between the scullery and the bakery. It was folded and hung on a nail. Through this door there is access to the inner courtyard, where on the opposite side there are the stables, the carriage house and the kennels. The kitchen maid saw the note after she had taken the dogs' food to the kennels, as she returned to the house. She took it down and, although she can hardly read, she realised that it was of urgent importance, so gave it to the housekeeper. The housekeeper brought it to me."

Holmes had closed his eyes, and appeared immersed in his thoughts, but as Lord Robartes finished, he asked at once: "Lord Robartes, have you placed charges with the police?"

"Yes, Mr. Holmes, but I have the feeling that we should not expect too much from them. You should be aware, gentlemen, that some five days ago at the home of the candidate of the Liberal Party, a waggon of manure was tipped into his well. The police seemed to regard this highly illegal act as no more than a tasteless prank, and made not the least attempt to find those responsible. I fear they will not help me either, as they scarcely looked at it and then gave it back to me."

"May I then please see the letter?" said Holmes.

Lord Robartes took it from his pocketbook, and gave it to my friend. Holmes first felt the paper carefully, held it against the light of the candle in the stand at his elbow, and then studied the written message. More to himself than to us, as it seemed, he murmured: "The paper used is of a good quality, but not the most expensive. The paper has neither a watermark, nor is it embossed by the manufacturer. The threat itself is formulated in a manner more that of an educated person. The clumsy capital letters are not only meant to threaten, but are also an attempt to conceal the handwriting. This may be the work of someone who fears that you may recognise his handwriting." Holmes looked up and addressed Lord Robartes clearly: "Should these criteria apply to the candidate of the Conservative Party, we may well have the author of this threat."

I saw how Lord Robartes was at first surprised, and then suddenly thought what this might mean. "Indeed, Mr. Holmes, you could be right. Dr. Moorman is proposed for the Tory Party, and I know his handwriting well. He is after all the veterinary specialist for all the livestock here at Lanhydrock. It is difficult to imagine that a man of his background would stoop to such a level, but passions run high. Tomorrow I will see him and challenge him. He will of course deny it, yet it could be so. His party has, Mr. Holmes, a difficult position here, and he has lost many friends. I have heard that he is, as a result of his probable election defeat, already suffering under the mental burden."

Lord Robartes was however interrupted, as my friend asked urgently, "Have you recently had to dismiss a servant?"

Holmes' unexpected question irritated him at first, but then Lord Robartes answered: "But yes, Mr. Holmes, ten days ago we had to dismiss a man. Why does that interest you, Mr. Holmes?"

Without waiting to answer, Holmes pressed further: "And this man had worked for a while as stable boy?"

Surprised, Lord Robartes replied: "Just so, Mr. Holmes, but how did you guess that?"

"That was no guess, Lord Robartes, but deduction!" and I saw that my friend was for a moment slightly nervous. Then he continued, calmly, as before: "It is clear that the stable boy, whom you had dismissed, deposited the threatening letter in Lanhydrock. Five points bring me to this conclusion:

1. The letter was left at a place where it must quickly be found. That shows that the messenger was familiar with the House.

2. The writer of the letter knew the messenger well enough to be sure that he could carry out his task as planned.

3. Your dogs, Sooty and Snowy are, as we observed yesterday on our arrival, effective watchdogs. Strangers are greeted on their approach with barking.

4. The dogs are kept in kennels alongside the stables, which are also on the other side of the bake house and scullery.

5. The messenger could place his letter without being observed.

These last three observations lead to a conclusion, that yesterday's fire was not an accident, but was set off by the dismissed stable boy."

Lord Robartes and I had followed this reasoning carefully, and it was the turn of Lord Robartes to speak up in appreciation. "Mr. Holmes, that was excellent. How simple it all seems, when you set it out for us! I will confront Dr Moorman directly tomorrow morning with this matter, and I will also search out some of his old invoices, which are probably on the same paper. Mr Jenkins can certainly find me something suitable. Dr. Moorman will undoubtedly suffer for it, but it is surely better so, than that he should come before the courts. I will however have to find a new veterinary surgeon."

Obviously delighted that the mystery of the threatening letter and the fire had been resolved, Lord Robartes had already risen, made his apologies and was about to leave, when he suddenly remembered that he had called Holmes to report on a quite different matter, and so he asked: "Mr. Holmes, has your visit today in Fowey already produced anything significant?"

"Not yet especially useful, Lord Robartes. I am coming to the conclusion that you need have no fears about the planned foundation stone laying. At the same time I have discovered something which has caught my interest, and into which I will need to investigate more deeply, before I can be more precise."

"Well, Mr. Holmes, I am sure that you will pursue your enquiries with just as much success as you have done with this letter. I bid you enjoy the evening, and please, of course, keep me informed about your progress."

With this he smiled again, and left us in the smoking room.

I had naturally intended to take Holmes to task, for going ahead alone in his investigations. It was however also clear to me that I had experienced a most relaxing and peaceful day out of doors, something which I had long not been able to enjoy. This was a reality which, together with my friend's impressive demonstration of deduction in respect of the threatening letter, allowed my earlier unease to resolve itself. Even so, after Lord Robartes had left us, there was a sense of oppressive silence, which I determined to break, by means of a question to Holmes.

"You have found in Fowey, then, no further indication of antagonism or threats against Lord Robartes and his charitable project, Holmes?"

"Just so, Watson. I must admit though, that I directed my attention principally to the late Mr Reeve, since he seemed to be the central figure of this matter."

"Who then did you visit today in Fowey?"

Although I attempted to ask in a completely dispassionate manner, my friend realised at once my disappointment that he had been making his enquiries alone. I sensed his searching look, as he replied: "My dear friend, you may be completely reassured about my journey to Fowey. I had in the first place to find out more about the late Mr. Reeve, as I had to build up this first picture, in order to know whether there is anything at all in this matter which deserves our attention." Holmes spoke warmly. I at once felt better; and as he now spoke again in the plural, this soon allowed any lingering doubt to disappear.

Interested, I asked again: "You remarked to Lord Robartes that you have indeed found something which retained your attention. May I perhaps ask what it was?"

"Naturally, Watson!"

I saw how a satisfied smile came to his lips, and his eyes lit up as he continued, in an emotionless voice: "But first let me tell you what I was doing today. To start, I visited the lawyer's chambers of which we had heard, to hear more about Mr. Ian Reeve. Mr. Edward Hoole turned out to be most friendly, but not a particularly communicative lawyer. I succeeded nevertheless in learning from him, that Mr. Reeve had been employed by him for some three years as a clerk. He had proved to be reliable, and in the case of research for legacies had particularly displayed a certain talent for investigations. Just half a year ago, Mr. Reeve had however to become more and more given to playing cards, with the result that he had lost more money than he could afford. It is therefore not surprising, that he came to be under pressure from his creditors. This was of course not conducive to the good name of the business, but it was also probably the reason why he attempted on Saturday 23rd August to gain access to the safe of the chambers. Mr. Hoole caught him there 'In flagrante delicto.' We, however, Watson, know what was in the safe at that time; it was the casket now belonging to Mrs. Ruth Lang, which clearly contained a fortune. Mr. Hoole dismissed Mr. Reeve summarily. I attempted to find out more about the affairs of Mrs. Lang, and especially the identity of her benefactor, but Mr. Hoole very properly maintained that discretion to which he is professionally obliged. He did however say that Mr. Reeve had been charged with telling the client that the affair had been successfully concluded. Thanks however to the indiscretion of Mr. Reeve, and to the good memory of the Rev. Carlyon, we have learned that the former owner of the casket is a Mr. Simon Osborn. There was a possibility therefore, that if Mr Reeve were required to report to Mr. Osborn on his progress, that then Mr. Osborn may have been lodging in one of the Fowey hotels, indeed, in one of the better hotels, if the casket were any guide. I therefore had some walking to do, and already at the third call I had a result.

With the assistance of some solid coin, I learned from the reception manager at the King of Prussia Hotel that Mr. Osborn hails from the New World, and that he had spent the whole of August at that hotel. My disappointment on learning that he had recently left, for an unknown destination, must have been apparent, for then he clearly felt obliged, with the aid again of the payment I made to him, at least to tell me what he had learned of Mr Osborne during his stay. Mr Osborn was an elderly man, always well-dressed, and yet whose hands and face had clearly been exposed to hard work and to every kind of weather. It had been obvious that he enjoyed the comforts of the hotel, but that he was unaccustomed to warm water to wash, or to the availability of fresh towels and bed linen. In the dining room, too, he often left an impression of being rather confused. Some guests were disturbed by his singular language, and by his obvious deafness. Other guests avoided him because of his erratic moods. But my informant suggested, kindly and perhaps not unreasonably, that he had may have been greatly fatigued by the rigours of an Atlantic crossing.

I had now learned far more than I had at first thought. I had at first hoped to find him in person and question him about Mr. Reeve. Since this was not now possible, I went to the address of Mr Reeve's former landlady, which Mr. Hoole had given me. There I learned that he had been a quiet tenant for most of his stay, but that he had in the last few months had difficulty in paying his rent. Finally, as she vigorously complained, two months' rent was still outstanding, and as he was now dead there was no way of obtaining this. She assured me repeatedly that she could not afford such a loss, but that she was pleased to have found a new tenant without delay. I then asked if there were any personal articles of Mr. Reeve still in the house. She explained that since she rented the rooms furnished, there was little, and items such as clothing she had passed on to the church bazaar. Then, however, she recalled that there were some books, and brought these at my request. The books revealed that his taste in literature was unimpressive. There was however among the books a small notebook, rather frayed and creased. I asked her to let me take this with me, and, aided by a sovereign which I gave her, she agreed. With this, I was now ready to return to Lanhydrock."

Holmes paused, and took from the inside pocket of his dinner jacket a small notebook and a pencil.

"And the notebook is of interest for our enquiries, Holmes?" I asked, now quite agitated.

"Yes, Watson, it is indeed. Firstly, all his information concerning Mrs. Ruth Lang, née Oakley, is here."

While Holmes said this, he turned over the pages, until he came to empty pages. I looked to see what he now had in mind. "What more does it tell us?" I asked impatiently.

"Here a page has been torn out" he said quietly.

"Is that all?" I asked, disappointedly. "How can that help us?"

"It may help us a great deal, my dear friend."

He looked across at me with mild humour as he began carefully to blacken the page he was holding, with his pencil. He explained as he did so: "The late Mr. Reeve appears to have pressed hard with his pencil as he wrote. In doing so, he has left an impression, invisible at first, on the next page. This invisible impression can, if we are careful, be brought out by gently blackening the page, so that the impression can be read." Holmes concluded his comment and held the darkened page in front of him. A satisfied smile followed, as he passed the notebook to me and turned to lighting his pipe. Curious, I read the blackened page, on which the following list was now visible:

Mr. Willoughby Pascoe	Banker, Lostwithiel
Mr. Jack Tonkin	Landlord, The Anchor in Gorran Haven
Mr. Reginald Dunstan	Merchant, St. Austell
Mr. Samuel Snell	Boat builder, Polperro

I looked questioningly to Holmes, but he would not be drawn further, preferring to sit with his pipe, deep in his thoughts. I would, as so often before, have to remain patient.

The next steps

The list which Holmes had found did not seem to me to have any bearing on the problems which Lord Robartes had described to us. Two of the names were quite unknown to us, although the other two were known and were indeed directly or indirectly connected with the building project of Lord Robartes. One had unexpectedly died; the other was at present not to be found. Who then were the other two persons named? Were they in some way to be connected to the project? And why were they on this list, and how did the late Mr. Reeve come to have such a list? And we only had an impression. Did the torn-out page still exist, and where might it be? The questions churned around in my head, so the sleep came only with difficulty.

Next morning, Holmes asked Lord Robartes whether the names of Jack Tonkin and Samuel Snell said anything to him. Rather as I suspected, both were quite unknown to him; and yet his answer disappointed me. Holmes, undisturbed, seemed to find this challenging and went on, "Then it looks very much as if we will have to search further. In view of the distance between the places on the list, it would appear necessary to spend a day or two away from Lanhydrock. In that case, to facilitate our enquiries it would be good to leave our luggage here, and to take with us only our light travelling bags."

"Please do whatever you consider necessary, Mr. Holmes. You know that you can rely upon my complete support."

And so it was, that we were soon again in the train, and on the way to St. Austell. During the journey I described to Holmes the extraordinary library at Lanhydrock House, and told him of my conversation with Lord Robartes concerning the impressive stone monuments of bygone cultures. It seemed I had awakened an interest in him, for he suddenly said that he would be pleased to visit these stone monuments. I was about to suggest that there may be, at the end of our enquiries, no obstacle to his doing so, when my attention was suddenly caught by a gleaming white object, which had come into view. This was a huge conical hill, and then I saw that on the gentle hills of the district there were more of these pyramids. Holmes broke into my surprise with some words of explanation.

"Would the name of William Cookworthy be familiar to you, my friend?"

It was not, as I truthfully replied, and looked expectantly at Holmes.

Clearly pleased, that he could again share his knowledge with me, he continued in explanation: "He was an apothecary, working in Plymouth, and had become known as a leading chemist as well as a pioneer in the manufacture of porcelain. You perhaps do not know that we owe the discovery leading to the manufacture of Chinese porcelain to a German? – No? – It was early in the last century that the alchemist Johann Friedrich Boettger in Dresden was attempting, under a mandate of the Elector of Saxony, to make gold. In this he was of course unsuccessful, but he incidentally discovered the secret of bone china. Most interesting, but I digress from my subject, William Cookworthy.

"Less that fifty years after the pioneering discovery by that German alchemist, Mr. Cookworthy discovered in the district of St. Austell extensive deposits of China clay, vital to porcelain manufacture. St. Austell has enjoyed as a consequence a remarkable economic prosperity. In is unfortunate that the excavated material contains some ninety per cent of waste material, with the result that these conical spoil heaps now dominate the landscape."

Fascinated, I had followed Holmes closely. I suspected that this knowledge resulted from his studies in chemistry. There was however no more time to ask, as we were arriving at St. Austell.

St. Austell station is on the hill above the town, and I was concerned about the unreliability of my leg, which had suffered a severe wound from a Jezail bullet in the Second Afghan War. I was therefore relieved that we found, not far from the station, a stable where we could hire a horse and carriage. We chose a gig, a one-horse open two-wheel carriage. Holmes took the reins, and once again I was surprised at the many talents he possessed. He steered our light carriage through the narrow streets of the small town with an almost professional agility, which I would not have considered possible.

We had soon reached our first call, the White Hart Hotel. This was the house into which Lord Robartes had seen Mr. Reeve enter. Clearly customers were not expected at this time, for a young boy, on hands and knees, was scouring the floor with a brush and white sand, and stopped abruptly to stare at us, as we entered. Behind the bar was a big, heavily built man, with a full beard and laughing eyes, who came to us and greeted us with a smile.

"Welcome to the White Hart, gentlemen. It will be a while before lunch is ready, but perhaps a tankard of my beer would help to pass the time?"

"Why, an excellent idea, my good man," replied Holmes with a friendly gesture.

The landlord was pleased to show us to a small table near the bar. As we took our places, Holmes turned to the landlord discreetly and said: "I would like to ask you one or two things, and I assure you that it will be to your advantage if you can spare us a little of your time."

With this, Holmes had drawn a sovereign from his waistcoat pocket, and laid it on the table. At first surprised, and then clearly impressed, at the prospect of reward, the landlord smiled and said: "Sir – just you ask. There are few guests at this time, and I have surely time for a chat."

"Wonderful, my good man…", but Holmes came no further, for the landlord laughed and said: "Just call me Peter, sir."

"Very good, Peter. And now, please bring for my friend, for me and for yourself a tankard, and come and join us."

Still rather puzzled, but clearly quite relaxed, the landlord brought our beer, sat down, raised his glass and said, "Your good health, gentlemen."

He took a deep draft, wiped his strong hand over his beard and looked at Holmes expectantly.

"Did you know the late Mr Reginald Dunstan?" asked Holmes.

"Why, yes, sir. He was a near neighbour here, though he did not himself frequent the White Hart. Indeed, he hardly ever left his house. They said he had a weak heart."

The landlord stopped respectfully. He looked for a moment at the coin on the table, and then spoke again. "That was what I also told the young man who came in here a short while ago, and also asked after Mr. Dunstan. He was not as generous as you are, sir."

I looked at Holmes, who took up again his questioning. :

"Did you know the young man?"

"No, sir, but I had seen him on various occasions hanging around here. I can't always take note of people on the street, but he was particularly conspicuous, with his red hair and the grey stripe. And then, one day, he came into the White Hart. He asked about the habits of old Mr. Dunstan, but I couldn't tell him much. I only really told him what I have told you. "

"But there is more?" asked Holmes.

"Well, yes, sir. He really wanted to know about Mr. Dunston's past life. I told him what most of us here knew."

"And what was that?" asked Holmes again.

"That the wealthy Mr Dunstan had started at the bottom and had worked his way up. As a young man he worked for the Caradon mine company."

"Caradon?" I asked, because I recalled that Lord Robartes had mentioned the name as we talked yesterday in the library. I had irritated Holmes, however, as his expression showed, by interrupting the landlord.

"Yes, sir, Caradon. Today Caradon is as lonely as is the Bodmin Moor above it, but it was once a famous copper mine. The mineworkers lived mostly around the mine, in cottages which were rented from the mine company. There they lived with their families, who often all worked for the mine. Eight-year-old lads would go down the mine, and the women and girls sorted out the stone blocks with the ore, and broke them up. They would work ten hours a day, and that for six days a week. In this hotel you can hear today the workers complain, who work to excavate China clay, but believe me, sir, it's not to be compared with the hardship of those old days. With forty they often could not work anymore, even when they lived that long. Many died early with consumption."

The landlord broke off to take another deep draft from his tankard. I was thinking of his words when Holmes directed another question to him.

"But Mr. Dunstan was not himself digging for copper ore underground, then?"

"That's right, sir, he was a storeman for the mine company"

"Storeman?" escaped my lips, and I again attracted the disapproval of Holmes, for interrupting the account.

"Yes, sir, it was like this, the miners had to buy their own supplies, tools, candles, even the black gunpowder they needed for blasting. They had to buy in the mine store, and that belonged to the company."

Now it was the turn of Sherlock Holmes to interrupt, as he said:

"It is a long road, Peter, from storeman to wealthy citizen. Do you know how it came about?

"We used to say that Mr. Dunstan kept close contact to the workers and the company, so that he knew which mines had the best yields, and where new mines were planned. He is supposed to have used what he knew to buy shares. Apart from that, he was supposed to have had shares in the Liskeard and Caradon Railway, which carried the copper away from the mines. I don't know if it's all true."

"But buying shares needs a certain starting capital?" I commented, and this time earned an approving nod from my friend.

"Surely, sir, but I don't know about that. Some always said, behind their hand, and now he's dead, that he once in the 1840s had a rich legacy, but others say that he was able, with his job, to supply the miners with tea, tobacco and spirits. That must have come from the smuggling. Fifty years ago the smuggling was the biggest business here on the south coast. However it came about, and long before it was obvious that the copper mines were becoming insolvent, Mr. Dunstan had already unloaded his shares and put his money in the China clay mines. In recent years he lived from his fortune. But there you are, sir, it's all hearsay."

"Thank you, Peter, your sovereign was well-earned," said Holmes in his friendliest way.

"Thank you, sir, and at your service." He picked up the gold coin, tucked it away, and asked: "And now may I propose a little lunch, gentlemen? We have the best steak and

kidney pie this side of Plymouth. And then another tankard?"
We accepted his proposal gratefully.

Our next visit was close to the brewery, where we soon found the ominous Fortuna Club, of which Mr. Tremayne had spoken. Inside the door was a reception table, behind which sat a heavily built man. Despite the smart jacket which he wore, he looked more coarse than cultivated, and his face displayed an uninviting grin. He introduced himself as Henry Nock, and congratulated us on our decision to patronise the club and grace it with our presence. His carefully worded recommendation of the club came to an abrupt end as Holmes made unmistakeably clear that we were not prospective new members. The fixed smile of Mr. Nock disappeared and was replaced by visible mistrust. "What are you looking for, then?" he growled. He stood up and his substantial frame towered threateningly over his desk.

"Information about Mr Pascoe" replied Holmes calmly.

"If you are friends of that man, then I'm glad you don't want to be a member here. And now, go back where you came from, out of here, or.....Damn it, Esther, what are you doing down here?" The young woman he had called

93

Esther had approached unobserved from the staircase leading to the first floor. She wore a light and most indiscreet dressing gown which seemed to reveal more of her person than it concealed.

She addressed Henry: "That one in number twelve: he's turned violent again, Henry." Mr Nock, letting out a violent expression which would have done justice to the East End of London, stamped off up the stairs. The young women was left standing there with us. She looked us up and down, and asked "New members?"

"No," I managed to say.

In search of help, I looked to Holmes, who was obviously quite unmoved by the tasteless attractions of this woman, and quietly asked, "Do you know Mr. Pascoe?"

A vulgar smile filled her face before she answered: "And who wants to know?"

"That is neither here nor there. But if you answer my question, this sovereign is yours." Holmes had once more taken the coin from his waistcoat pocket, and the young woman looked at it hungrily, and then nervously back at the stairs. Back with us, she spoke in a scarcely audible voice, and whispered: "Mr. Pascoe has been a member of the club for years. He often loses at cards, but he can afford it. That old man is rolling in money. He often uses our services upstairs, although he really prefers boys. But he so often breaks out into violence, that there is always trouble."

"When did you last see him?"

"That was a while back. He was here with a young man, and they seemed to understand one another very well, if you see what I mean. He wanted to rent a room for the two of them, but we don't do that here. That made him angry again, and I thought, now there'll be a fight. But the young one calmed him down finally, and I think I heard him suggest that they go together to Liskeard."

"Who was his companion? Did you hear his name? Or perhaps you can describe him?"

The young woman looked quickly upstairs, before she whispered: I don't know his name, but he has fiery red hair with two grey stripes, and I had noticed him. He played cards a few times, but always came and left alone. Just that last time – he left the club with the old man. That's all."

Suddenly she snatched up the sovereign, and hastened to the staircase.

"Come, Watson, we will learn nothing more here." With these words, he turned and walked out, and I hastened to follow him. During our return to the stables, to give back the pony and gig, I resolved that I would prefer to tell my beloved Mary nothing of this episode. I hope moreover, as I write these notes, that my description will in no way offend the propriety and finer feelings of my deeply respected readers.

As soon as we had returned our carriage, and had collected our travelling bags from the 'Left Luggage,' Holmes told me that we would now take the first train to Liskeard. I had no chance to ask him more as we had to buy tickets, and were pleased already to hear the snorting and hissing of an approaching train as we climbed the steps of the elaborate cast iron footbridge which graces St. Austell station, to reach the eastbound platform.

After finding a seat in a first-class compartment, and as the train set off, I asked my friend: "Holmes, what are you thinking of doing next?"

"As I said to Lord Robartes this morning, we must find out more about the persons on our list. That was why we made the visit to St. Austell, which incidentally proved to be most instructive."

I had to admit privately that to describe our visit to St. Austell, and especially to the Fortuna Club, a quite different adjective might seem appropriate. But rather than say so, I asked: "Would it not have been better to ask Mr. Pascoe's housekeeper about his disappearance?"

"No, Watson, I think not. What she could tell us is what she has already told Lord Robartes. In Liskeard, however, we may be able to pick up the trail of Mr. Pascoe again. And should that not be so, Liskeard is still the best point from which to make a visit to the boat-builder, Samuel Snell in Polperro. Otherwise we would have had to return with the train, and take a local train to Fowey, and cross the river by ferry to Bodinnick. To reach Polperro, we would still have had to hire a horse and trap. It will be easier to start from Liskeard."

Holmes broke off and began to fill his pipe again. I had in the meantime, thanks to the sketch map I had made earlier, some familiarity with the country, and could thus easier follow his detailed comment. I also thought we would be better served in Liskeard, and so remarked: "That would have been a most complicated journey, and would surely take much longer."

"Quite so, Watson, and the tides in the Fowey River affect the ferry service."

I had nodded in agreement, but, interesting as these details were, my hope that he might tell me more about his plans in Liskeard were to be disappointed. Clearly he preferred to sit quietly with his pipe, immersed in his own thoughts. I found my book in my travel bag, and began to read. It was, as I discovered, not easy to concentrate, as my thoughts kept going back to our enquiries in St. Austell, and especially to that most curious establishment, the Fortuna Club. I was relieved when our train reached Liskeard, where we alighted to find a convenient hotel.

Smugglers and Wreckers

Once established in the King's Arms Hotel, I used the time before dinner to write my notes of our case so far. Holmes had gone to telegraph all the Liskeard hotels and guest houses, in the hope that he would perhaps in that way obtain information on the movements of Mr. Pascoe or of Mr. Reeve. It would be the following day, at the earliest, before he would know how successful he might be. Since our visits in St. Austell, Holmes had said conspicuously little about the matter in hand. As a friend of many years' standing, I knew what this meant. I knew that he would not prematurely speculate concerning the outcome of a case. His view was that if one were tempted to do so, it would result in subsequent enquiries tending to seek only those facts which supported the first suspicion. When, therefore, he returned to the hotel, I avoided talking about the case, and we enjoyed a quiet evening in that most agreeable surrounding.

After breakfast, the next morning, we again hired a pony and gig and took the road to Polperro. We had hardly left Liskeard when I asked: "Holmes, did you receive any replies to your telegram enquiries of yesterday evening?"

"I did indeed, Watson. By all appearances, neither Mr. Pascoe nor Mr. Reeve has ever lodged in Liskeard."

"Might they not have registered under a false name?"

"That is a wise observation, Watson. I had had the same idea, and so I had included with my telegram a description of Mr. Reeve's conspicuous hair. But all was in vain."

"Could it perhaps be that, that... that young woman Esther at the Fortuna Club misled us?"

"That is naturally possible. She had however no advantage from doing so. Why should she?"

I did not have an answer to this, so we continued in silence. I was pleased that Holmes had again taken the reins, for travelling in Cornwall, even on the principal roads, is no light-hearted undertaking. The road had been made up, but was very narrow, and often in poor condition. This was particularly unpleasant as we had some steep hills, both up and down, to negotiate. Driving the gig demanded Holmes' full concentration, and so I chose now not to distract him with my questions, but rather to devote my attention to the countryside. Even this was, however, more easily said than done, for we found ourselves often on deeply sunken ways, with steep banks on either side, which were often so far overgrown with bushes and ancient stunted trees, as to form a leafy natural tunnel over our heads. This naturally prevented me from seeing very much, but where the growth was thinner, and the banks fell away, I had a view over rolling meadows, woods and pastures, or sometimes harvested fields, which were also separated by high, weather-beaten hedges.

It was almost midday as we arrived in Polperro. This small fishing village is at the mouth of a narrow river valley, formed by the River Pol. The houses are therefore built on the steep slopes on both sides. We approached the harbour through a maze of narrow alleyways. There we found a smithy and stable, where we could leave our pony and gig in safety. From there we continued on foot. I delighted in the sunshine, which was still warm, despite the advanced season. Over us wheeled and screeched the seagulls, and there was overall a smell of fish, seaweed and salty seawater. The harbour appeared suddenly at our feet. As we arrived at low water, the harbour itself was almost free from water, and the boats lay on their keels in the mud. Despite an apparently meaningless confusion of nets, lines, ropes, heavy anchors and chains, or perhaps because of all these things, the harbour, surrounded by densely nestling houses, appeared remarkably picturesque. We soon found Samuel Snell's boatyard, for a large new sign advertised it. Alongside the shed, in which there lay three half-completed hulls, with five workmen obviously hard at work on them, we found a separate building housing the office and a store with various articles for the work. We entered, and a small bell over the door announced us. From the back of the room there emerged a middle-aged man, who came briskly to meet us.

He welcomed us in friendly style and asked: "Good day, gentlemen. How can I help you? Would you be thinking of commissioning a new boat?"

Without giving a reply, Holmes asked directly:

"Would you be Mr. Samuel Snell, the owner of this yard?"

"That, sir, I am indeed."

"Well, my name is Sherlock Holmes, and this is my friend Dr Watson. We would like to ask you some questions."

Agreeably, without showing any sign that he might have recognised our names, Mr. Snell nodded his agreement.

"Do the names Willoughby Pascal, Jack Tonkin, or Reginald Dunstan mean anything to you?" asked Holmes.

"Well now, most of our people here know Willoughby Pascoe, and they all say he is a disagreeable man, and where loans are concerned, even more of a skinflint than was his father. I've never met him personally, and so that's only what they say. The other names mean nothing to me. But may I ask you something, Mr. Holmes?"

"Naturally, Mr. Snell, please go ahead."

"Why are you asking about these three persons in particular?"

"That is soon explained. An acquaintance of ours is recently deceased. In his estate, which we are managing, we have found a note on which stood your name and these other three persons", answered Holmes, slightly at variance with the truth.

Mr. Snell looked at us in great surprise, and then said: "That is surely strange, for as I say, I know them not. And yet, it could perhaps be... no, that must surely be impossible."

We looked at him searchingly, and asked Mr. Snell to continue. He did so, after some hesitation and somewhat uneasily: "Just for a moment I thought of my uncle, whose name I also have. But I would not for a moment think that anyone would connect my uncle with Mr Pascoe."

"Really?" asked Holmes.

It was obvious that Mr. Snell felt that my friend was not really following him, for he went on to explain what he meant.

"You should know more about them, gentlemen, to understand why. Both my father, God rest his soul, and my uncle were, as lads here, fishermen. But they soon went separate ways. My father was a capable workman, and soon found a job with a boat-builder. My uncle went to sea, was long away from home, and then, when he came back, found himself doing, let's say, less creditable things. He liked to tell the tales later, of when he had been a smuggler."

He interrupted his account with an almost embarrassed smile, and then he continued:

"That was in Polperro nothing new. At that time the whole village lived from smuggling. It's naturally all finished now, and today most people here live from the fishing. The men go out in their boats, just like I build them here, and the women and most of the children clean and salt the fish for packing, in the three fish factories which are close by us here. All that can recall the smuggling today are the caves in the cliff walls, where they hid their goods, and there are still many secret passages under the houses where they could bring the wares away. My uncle could tell some good stories, but, I am glad to say, he was never a wrecker".

As Mr. Snell again paused, I took the lead and asked: "Why, what was a wrecker, Mr. Snell?"

"That was what they called the really evil ones who fell on the many ships that stranded on this coast. They plundered the cargo, and even the ships themselves, often regardless of the cries for help of the drowning sailors. Some of them went so far as to light false fires and signals, so as to mislead the seamen and guide the ships onto the rocks, so as to plunder them. Those were truly wicked people, and I am relieved that my uncle was not among them. It was back in 1846 that my father started his own boatyard, with my uncle as partner, and that is where you are now. It was a great achievement to make the jump from fisherman to boat-builder, but it certainly isn't the world in which a Mr Pascoe is to be found."

"Mr. Snell, this is all most interesting, and I thank you for it. May I perhaps speak with your uncle personally?" said Holmes.

"I am deeply sorry, sir, but that is not possible. My uncle died, on the night of September the seventh."

"Oh, my sincere sympathy, Mr. Snell," I said and again earned a disapproving glance from Holmes.

"Thank you, sir, you are very kind", said Mr. Snell, turning to me. He then continued, facing us both: "To tell the truth, my grief has its limits. My uncle, even as my father was still alive, was never an easy man to live with. He would sometimes, without a word to anyone, go off out to sea for several days, or he would search out his old mates in a disreputable public house somewhere around the coast. The business was all in my father's hands, and as he died, I took it over myself."

Again, Mr. Snell paused, and shook his head somewhat bitterly.

"And yet ... despite your uncle's character, your father was able to build up your business with him", suggested Holmes.

"True, sir, and even when I was a lad it had always surprised me. I had asked my father, and one day he explained that we owed a great debt of gratitude to my uncle. It was he who had advanced to my father the money, to realise his dream of setting up the boatyard, and my father, a good man, was ready to set aside in return the misdeeds of my uncle. After my father's death, I did the same. And my uncle, with age and time, became a little quieter. He still went off out to sea, but he was then usually happy to warm up again in the evening at the Three Pilchards."

"The Three Pilchards?" I asked. .

"Why yes, sir, that's the inn and guest house across the harbour, just before the breakwater, a fine house, and my uncle loved it. Almost every night he would be there, and seldom came home before midnight. And that was his undoing…"

We look up sharply and Mr. Snell continued, with a shake of the head.

"On the night of September the seventh, he had again been drinking hard. Trying to find his way home, he got tangled up in a pile of nets. It looks as if he struggled to get free, came too close to the edge of the quay, and fell in the harbour. With the nets he dragged down a small anchor and chain, couldn't free himself, and so drowned. They found his body next morning at low water."

For a moment silence fell. Holmes was first to move; he took two sovereigns from his waistcoat pocket, and addressed Mr. Snell, saying: "Thank you for all that you have been able to tell us. It was most helpful. I hope you will find this an adequate compensation for the time you have most generously given us "

Mr. Snell thanked him warmly and made a slight bow, and Holmes turned to me to say, "Come, Watson, I think it is time to think of our own lunch, and with Mr Snell's recommendation I can think of no better place that the Three Pilchards."

Loud conversation, and laughter, tobacco smoke and the smell of beer hung in the air of the Three Pilchards. As we entered, however, the natural suspicion towards unexpected strangers, still strong in a village that had long lived from smuggling, brought an immediate silence. It was only after the landlord had led us to a table in the rear of the room that the disturbance which we had obviously caused seemed again to give way to a more relaxed atmosphere. The landlord's name was Thomas, and he enthusiastically praised his speciality, his fish pie, which, as he explained was a fish stew with baked covering of mashed potatoes. A short while later we were enjoying a hearty and robust meal which thoroughly justified his recommendation. While we were eating many guests had finished, and were leaving the inn, which was soon nearly empty. As we finished our meal, and when we appeared to be the only remaining guests, Holmes did the same as at the White Hart in St. Austell, inviting the landlord to take a tankard with us and help us with our questions.

"We have been told that old Samuel Snell from the boatyard was a regular guest in the Three Pilchards. Is that so, Thomas?"

"Oh, yes, sir, Samuel came here every day."

"And he always went home late?"

"Late? You can say so, sir, old Samuel only went home when I closed up at night. He sat every evening at the same table, and drank his beer. And then he told his tales, to anyone who would listen, of his days as a daring sailor. His adventures were always exciting, and I heard bits of them as I went about my work. Now and again he would talk about the old smuggling days, when he was always the courageous and crafty one who led the Coast Guards a dance. Some of his tales were surely enriched with a generous portion of sailors' yarns."

"And he was here on the night he died, in the Three Pilchards?"

The landlord took a good draft. "Yes, sir, he had drunk heavily that night, more spirits than beer. It was sad, for he had had a very good evening. There was a stranger here, who obviously enjoyed old Samuel's stories. The stranger was generous, and as the first brandy bottle was empty, he ordered another. After the stranger had left, Samuel drank what was left in the second bottle. It was soon after midnight, and time to close. I helped Samuel to the door, and he could hardly stand. I half expected he would sleep it off there by the door, but it seems he tried to get home, and fell in the harbour. That's where they found him, dead, next morning."

"Can you perhaps describe the stranger who had kept company with Mr. Snell? Did he have a prominent head of hair?" asked Holmes with interest.

The landlord thought for a moment, and then replied.

"No, sir, nothing like that. His hair was grey, like many another old man, and I thought he had already drunk before coming here. As he came into the Three Pilchards, he was already unsteady on his pins. But he could carry a lot, evidently, for his walk was no worse when he left."

"Thank you, Thomas, for your great help, said Holmes. This sovereign is yours."

"Always at your service, I'm sure, sir, and would you like another glass?"

We declined graciously, as it was already time to think of our return to Liskeard.

I had greatly enjoyed our journey to the sea, and my thoughts now lingered over that apparently sleepy and peaceful fishing village. You will, dear reader, surely not wonder, that Holmes and I, during the return journey, sat for some time in silence together. But then the moment seemed ripe to ask him the question that had occupied me, ever since we left Lanhydrock, and which seemed now, after our visit to Polperro, still to be relevant. "Holmes, have our enquiries brought us any further, in respect of our problem?"

"That, Watson, depends on which problem you have in mind. For that which troubled Lord Robartes, we have found no indications at all. The concern he felt for the safety of his sponsors and guests, and those who are supporting his project, seems not to be confirmed. My focus had however already shifted to the list which we had discovered, and to that problem I can say that we have come nearer to it. Between the persons on the list there are emerging a number of common features."

This irritated me somewhat, as I could see nothing in common, between a boat-builder, a merchant, an innkeeper and a banker. I asked therefore, rather sceptically, "Really?"

It was some time before Holmes began with his explanation.

"It is certainly too early to advance a hypothesis, for we still have a fourth name, on the list, of a person of whom we know nothing. Even so, I will outline to you what we know already:

1. Mr. Willoughby Pascoe is, like his father, a banker. He is however following his father not only by profession. As was his father, he is also a merciless man who tends to aggression. In his private life he displays one or two distinctly unusual tendencies. That Mr. Pascoe can conduct his life in such a manner must surely be due to his social status and his substantial fortune.

2. Mr. Reginald Dunstan, the merchant, was once a storeman at the Caradon mining company. The knowledge he acquired there, and a reputed inheritance, sometime after 1840, have however permitted him to make investments and to become a wealthy man.

3. Mr. Samuel Snell began life as a fisherman, sailor and smuggler. In 1846 he sets up a boatyard with his brother in Polperro. The necessary capital comes from … Samuel Snell.

4. Mr. Pascoe, but also Mr. Dunstan and Mr. Snell, are all elderly men.

Does anything particular strike you, old friend?"

Holmes looked at me with interest, but my thoughts were clearly too slow for him, for he started again, with emphasis:

"Both Mr. Snell, and Mr. Dunstan had a considerable fortune in the eighteen-forties. Mr. Dunstan had allegedly an inheritance. Can that be true? And as for Mr. Snell, did the money which he gave his brother really come from smuggling?"

"I cannot see, really, Holmes, what this might all have to do with Mr. Pascoe. Or, wait a moment, do you think that Mr Snell and Mr Dunstan received their money from Mr. Pascoe?"

"Just so, Watson."

"But what would prompt him to such an act?"

"To that, I can only study the options I see, but it seems to me that his violent character, and his somewhat unconventional lifestyle, may be at the bottom of it, because these have surely brought him on many occasions into difficulties. Such persons are often all too ready to use their money, as long as it lasts, to get out of trouble. But to say any more must wait at least until we have had an opportunity to visit the fourth person on our list. Any more must remain purely speculation."

I had followed Holmes and his explanation with some doubt, as it seemed unusually farfetched. I began to fear that my friend was in reality frustrated by the failure to find anything more which might relate to Lord Robartes' fears. Now, instead of admitting it, he seemed to be constructing an elaborate case around the list which we had obtained from Mr. Reeves' notebook. Had Holmes' disposition and attitudes been more balanced, I might have challenged him there and then. But I chose to remain silent; and it was getting dark, and I looked forward to the warmth and security of our hotel. To this there now came a weather change. That gentle breeze which we had noted in Polperro had now given way to a stiff, cool wind, even though we were now again travelling further inland. Tired as I was, and with my head full of queries and contradictions, I tried to keep warm in my heavy coat.

A gruesome discovery

The fresh breeze, which I had found rather disagreeable in the evening air, was still present on the Sunday morning. Moreover, the train service, on a Cornish Sunday, permitted no great opportunity to move on. We therefore sought again to hire a gig, although that also was not necessarily easy. It seemed however that word had gone around in Liskeard, that we were seeking something. The owner of the stables had heard in discussion, over the inn-table, that we were not the only strangers who had hired a carriage at this otherwise rather quiet season; Some days earlier, an elderly man, not from those parts, had taken a wagon, with two horses, an unusual hiring at this time, and had gone up the road towards Minions on Bodmin Moor. Holmes listened, apparently disinterested, and assured the stable owner that we needed nothing more than a gig and pony. He turned to me to suggest that we might also make an instructive trip up to "The Hurlers" near Minions. The journey led us once again along narrow lanes, often bordered by high hedges and bushes. A view to the side was rarely possible, and when it was, we saw rolling fields, mostly already harvested, divided by the thick hedges, and occasionally we saw whitewashed farmhouses.

The road soon began to climb, and I was relieved that Holmes was satisfied to drive. I therefore took his map and concentrated upon finding the way. A first stop, and a rest for us as well as for the pony, came as we reached Trethevy Quoit. This stone monument from ancient times was most impressive. I recalled my conversation in the library with Lord Robartes, and how he had described it to me with the aid of the book by William Borlase. I told Holmes what I had learned, and it was with obvious interest that he examined both exterior and interior of Trethevy Quoit in close detail. The thought occurred to me, that our stay in Liskeard might not be to pursue our enquiries, but simply to satisfy Holmes' wish to see for himself Trethevy Quoit and The Hurlers. The thought did not trouble me long, for his real interest also pleased me, as did the fact that I was at least in this way able to help him.

During our stop, the sun had broken through the clouds and began to warm us again. The road before us, as we set off again, was still climbing, but less steeply than earlier; and this gave Holmes, whose concentration was no longer fixed upon driving our gig, the opportunity to reflect aloud.

"There are in Cornwall many remains and traces from earlier, long-vanished peoples, and the condition of these, where they have been excavated, is truly remarkable. You will know, Watson, that such monuments are often today hidden, underground, so that one perhaps only sees an unusually shaped mound. But what have you learned, old friend, about the purpose of such huge stone monuments?"

"I had read in the book of Borlase that they are considered to be burial places. "

"Most interesting, Watson. I would like to have known whether the positions and alignment of these stones was of a particular significance, or indeed if the hole in the roof stone were there for a purpose. Truly, these stone monuments are even more mysterious than the many singular earth ramparts in these parts, which seem to bear witness to far-off prehistoric rivalries. "

He paused for a moment, and then continued with enthusiasm: "Cornwall is truly a land of legends and myths. Think only of Tintagel Castle, where they say that King Arthur was born, or Slaughterbridge near Camelford, where he is reputed to have fought his last battle. On the north slopes of Bodmin Moor lies Dozmary Pool, into which Sir Bedivere threw Excalibur, Arthur's sword, so that it might be taken back by the Lady of the Lake".

I had followed with fascination Holmes' observations. Before I could make any further remark, however, the landscape took a sudden turn, presenting to our sight a quite different panorama. My attention was completely absorbed, as we came onto a plateau, free from trees and hedges, and as we rolled over it, we were quite unprotected from the wind. The conspicuously dominant granite outcrop of Caradon Hill rose out of the level foreground. On our right the view was occupied by the remains of innumerable stone engine houses, with their great chimneys, flanked by steep slopes of stone debris. In contrast, on the left was a gently rising moorland hillside, covered with heathland and gorse, and ferns which were already turning brown. All seemed lonely and abandoned, as did even the handful of sheep grazing on the open moor. Looking carefully, I discovered a distant church tower, and soon a number of farmhouses came into sight. There soon appeared some rows of low cottages, which appeared empty. I realised that this must be the mining village of Minions, of which the landlord of the White Hart in St. Austell had told us.

On the west side of the village we discovered a farmer, who was happy, even on a Sunday, to care for our pony and gig for a few coins. He was friendly and helpful, and at once showed us the way to the Hurlers. Holmes and I set off on foot on the path. We had covered scarcely more than a few yards, in this moorland, when we came over a low ridge and discovered the three great stone circles directly before us. The drawings of William Borlase had, as far as I could tell, given a most accurate overview of that which we now found before us. It was a completely absorbing spectacle, and I was at once struck by the question, to what purpose such a construction might have been undertaken. Holmes did not wait. He set off at a determined pace, to come nearer to the great stone circles and to see them better. I could not at first follow him, and when I did catch up again, I was more than thankful to sit on a fallen stone of the middle of the three circles. I could thus take the weight off my leg, which had already, with its old wound, become most painful.

The wind was now, in this exposed place, quite severe, and I wrapped up warmly. Holmes seemed not to notice the weather, for he was walking from one stone to another, in order to take everything in. After spending some time in the third stone circle, he called back to me, that he wanted to see the Cheesewring, the granite hill above the rings. I called back, wishing him well, but it took, in the wind, at the distance involved, several attempts before he understood. Holmes was obviously planning to be away for some time, so I decided to move, to keep off the cold. On the way from Minions to the stone circles, we were close to one of the mine engine houses, and nearby I had seen a pond which interested me. I went to look at it more closely.

The water in this pond was deep brown in colour, and from close up was somewhat repellent. The banks were however full of reeds and rich, thickly woven grass, and had a wildly romantic air. A little way on I found a gorse bush, bent like the reeds by the strong wind. I had stood some time studying these natural features, but now, as I came to move again, with a step sideways, I found that my tracks in the turf had filled at once with water. Another brisk gust of cold wind swept over the moor and left me shivering. Or might it be the melancholy moorland, which had this effect on me? I decided to move again and this time went to look more closely at the engine house which we had seen on the way.

The square tower, and the tall chimney, visible from afar, were massively built. Not only the form, but the building materials, enhanced this effect. The engine house, now abandoned, was built of heavy granite blocks, and had a gabled roof of slates. As I came nearer, I saw that the upper part of the chimney, and the arches of the window places, were also of slate. I learned only later the function of these buildings was to house a large steam engine which provided the power needed to pump water out of the mine, and also to drive with belts the hammers used to break the ore dug out in the mine. It would also drive the hoists which were used by the miners to descend into, and climb out of, the mine. These, I learned, are still used in Cornwall in places today. They consist of a wooden pole, with horizontal platforms secured to it, which moves up and down in the mine shaft. The miners go down the mine by stepping off the platform after each vertical move, onto a side platform fixed to the mine wall, and then back onto the vertical stepladder at its next downward move. There is also a much more efficient double lift which has two vertical wooden stepladders serving two sets of platforms. The single lift was very often favoured, as the vertical mine shafts, which go to the bottom of the mine, are often narrow. I knew nothing of all this on that cold autumn day on Bodmin Moor, but the fascination had hold of me, as my curiosity drove me to see for the first time into the interior of an engine house. I looked through the window frame.

It was not in fact easy to see anything, in the darkness inside the building. The room seemed quite empty, except for a stool lying on the floor. No doubt the owners, when the mine closed, had removed everything which might still be of value. I was about to turn away, when something on the stool caught my eye. There was something there, shining intermittently, as a shaft of sunlight came and went. There was perhaps a hole in the tiled roof which allowed sunshine to enter and momentarily light up the darkness. I was at once curious, and still feeling the cold, so I determined, if I could get in, to see for myself, in the engine house. The door was not bolted, so I went in. The door allowed more light to enter, and also some fresh air, which helped me because the air inside was not only full of damp and decay, but had a most disturbing smell. I took a few moments as my eyes adjusted to the darkness. I approached the stool, to see what had been laid on it. It was a small leather travelling bag, which had a gold-coloured metal fastener, reflecting the light, surely what had caught my attention. This bag had not been here very long, as it was scarcely dusty, whereas everything else was thick with a heavy coat of dust. This irritated me, for could it be that someone was using this abandoned engine house as a shelter? As my eyes followed the outlines in the room, I now saw footsteps in the dust. They led to the back corner, and suddenly I realised that there were the outlines of two feet. Now, if this was a place where tramps and vagabonds came to shelter, the wise thing was surely to leave it again, as quickly as possible. And yet... as a doctor something in me said that there might here in the back corner be someone needing help. I resolved to go nearer and speak to him.

"Excuse me! Can I help you?" I said, in a voice which did not ring quite as resolute as I had intended.

I was now nearer the corner of the room, and the disagreeable smell which I had noticed on entering the engine house had now given way to a repulsive, evil stench. I felt the hairs on my neck prickle. I knew this smell all too well. I pulled out my pocket handkerchief to hold it protectively over nose and mouth. Carefully, I looked more closely. There was a body lying on the floor. I could not see clearly in the darkness, but I picked out the outline of a man who lay on his side, with his back to me. A sudden movement made it appear that his chest rose and fell. Against my better judgment I pressed nearer, to see he was bound hand and foot, with a sack drawn over his head. I bent to release him, and then with repulsion saw that the movement of his chest came, not from his breathing, but from several disgusting rats which had fallen upon the body. My presence had briefly disturbed them, so that they had drawn back, and left something behind which was hardly to be recognised as a human being. Nauseated, I reeled backwards, and knew I had not been mistaken at the fearful smell.

That which was left of the body was already far decomposed. I have as a doctor seen death in many forms. This stench and the decaying, half-gnawed body, however, took me directly back to my military service in Afghanistan. And I had begun to feel that I was safe from those awful past scenes of tortured comrades, of soldiers whom I, as a doctor, had been no more able to help, and whose only deliverance from their suffering lay in death. Those scenes filled my vision again, pictures I had hoped and struggled to put far behind me. Now they were here, in this place, as real and immediate as ever. The feeling rose in me that I must suffocate in this dark engine house. My stomach was seized by cramps, and my throat seemed strangled. I wanted to get away, leave the engine house and run, anywhere, but I was helpless. My legs gave way, and I was seized by panic. My heart was racing, and I heard my blood pulsing in my ears. However much I knew I had to leave this grisly scene, I could not tear my eyes away from the dead man.

A hand gripped hard on my shoulder. Someone had crept up behind me, unobserved, and unheard. Was I about to meet the same fate as the man on the floor? The idea broke through the helplessness, which had left me lame and terrified. I struck the hand brutally away, heavily as it lay on me, and turning, struck out as quickly as I could. I was ready to fight for my life!

In the half-darkness I saw the face of my opponent, and in an indescribable relief, saw that it was Holmes, who had followed my steps. I sighed deeply, and with the relief my whole body relaxed, as my legs became again weak beneath me. Holmes, watching and observing as always, saw my condition and commanded, in a voice which tolerated no argument,

"Watson, come outside with me at once!"

With these words he laid his muscular arm around my back and led me back into the open. The cold wind, which a short while before so chilled me, now seemed refreshing and clean. Leaning on Holmes, I managed to make the way back to the farmhouse where we had left the pony and gig. I remember that Holmes told the farmer, in a few words, that we had discovered a body in the engine house. More than that is very vague to me. I had only a very unclear feeling that Holmes had gone back with the farmer to the engine house. I remained in the care of the farmer's wife, with a glass of brandy.

Holmes and I finally set out in the gig, back to Liskeard, at first in total silence. I had recovered to some degree from the shock which the experience had given me, but I could not find words to talk to Holmes. I was, truth to tell, also ashamed of my own weakness. I feared that Holmes would surely be disappointed that I had failed in a critical situation. This thought obsessed me on the way back, until I broke out and suddenly said: "Holmes, I really have to ask your forgiveness for my behaviour this afternoon."

Although he wanted nothing more than to get back to Liskeard as quickly as possible, he stopped the pony and looked at me curiously. "Whatever do you mean, Watson?"

I swallowed hard, before I could begin to say what troubled me. "My behaviour, as I saw the dead man in the engine house, was quite irresponsible. I felt as weak and helpless as a child. When such a moment as this suffices to bring me so deplorably out of balance, what might it be like when a really threatening moment is upon us? In such a situation I can scarcely be of any help to you, but rather a useless burden."

"My dear friend, you are far too severe with yourself. As you found the body this afternoon you were totally unprepared, and I am certain that the condition it was in reminded you directly of your time as a military doctor."

Here he stopped, and looked at me with that penetrating studious expression of which his keen eyes were capable. I had at once the feeling that he saw deep into my soul. I felt my feeling confirmed, as he continued:

"You have told me, and as far as I know, others, practically nothing of your military service. And what you have said, is, as so often when soldiers return from their battlefields, relatively light-hearted. None of these home-comers relate the pain, suffering, fear or death they have seen and experienced. Nor do you, Watson. Be that as it may, I find it in no way remarkable, that you were suddenly, in this moment, as you discovered the corpse, thrown off balance. You may see weakness, but for me it reflects, in truth, the strength of your character."

I looked in surprise at Holmes, and he went on to explain:

"In spite of all that you have seen and had to experience in your life, you still have a generous and sympathetic heart. In spite of all the evil of this world, you still go out openly and honestly to those you meet. You have a keen sense of justice and an incomparable loyalty. Should I ever be in a life-and-death situation, I could not imagine a better person to have at my side than you, my dear friend. And now stop this preoccupation with your own self-doubt, and let us concentrate on what we must do next."

With these words, Holmes turned abruptly from me, and set the pony and gig in motion again. His friendly words were balm to me, and banished all my anxiety. In the whole time, a long time, that I had now known my friend, I had seldom had a chance to see so deeply into his heart, as I had now done on this cold autumn afternoon in Cornwall. His sympathy, which I had never expected, had greatly moved me, and I sat for a while in silence beside him. But now the way was less steep, and Holmes could relax a little from the full concentration which had up to now been required. I spoke to him again. "Holmes, have you already an idea, who the dead man in the engine house might be?"

"From that which is left of the body, it will scarcely be possible to arrive at a clear identification, and yet I believe it to be the body of the missing banker, Willoughby Pascoe."

I nodded thoughtfully. Truth to tell, I had already had the same idea. Before I could say so, however, Holmes gave me his own explanation.

"Leading to this conclusion, I take first the travelling bag which was close to the body. Its contents correspond closely to the description which Mr. Pascoe's housekeeper gave to Lord Robartes. The linen and the pocket handkerchiefs, and the bag itself, carry the monogram W.P. This monogram was also on the clothes he had worn. The dead man's suit, before the rats had fallen upon it, had been of an unusually high quality. Moreover, as I examined the body, I found that his pocket watch was a quite exquisite example. Engraved on the outside of the cover were also again the initials W.P., and as I let the cover spring open, I could see the engraved dedication

Money is power!

Your father

Bartholomew Pascoe, 1845

All these indications led me to one conclusion. Naturally, the objection might be made, that it is a different person, and that an attempt had been made to suggest it is the missing banker. That would demand an answer to more questions. Who would want to do that? And why? And who might it otherwise be? As you see, Watson, that does not help us. For the present, I will continue to work on the conclusion that this was the body of Willoughby Pascoe."

I was fascinated by Holmes' account, although I was struck cold by the thought that he had carefully analysed the corpse in the rat-infested engine house. To escape from these thoughts, I remarked: "Then Mr. Pascoe was kidnapped, and brought to that lonely engine house, so that he could be concealed there. Then, however, the excitement and the arduous journey were too much, and he died before he might be ransomed."

"Your hypothesis is not too far out, Watson. There is though, an important consideration which speaks against it."

"And what could that be?"

"Caring for a prisoner over a longer period requires that regular visits should be made, or even, that someone was on watch in the engine house. Either of these would, in such an environment, at once attract attention. And as you will surely agree, Watson, that is exactly what a kidnapper would not desire."

"But Holmes, that would mean that an unknown person had deliberately brought Mr. Pascoe to the engine house, in the intention of leaving him to a dreadful death", I burst out, very shocked. I looked at Holmes anxiously. What sort of brutal person might that have been, to be capable of such an evil act?

Holmes seemed to read my thoughts, as he replied: You have there a central point, which must help to lead our focus towards the murderer. My second visit to the engine house allowed me to obtain some thoroughly interesting facts concerning the unknown person. Mr. Pascoe was hobbled and bound hands and feet with ropes. Moreover, he was secured, to a metal ring in the wall of the engine house, with another rope around his waist. Examination of these revealed that they had been made fast with a clove hitch and a round turn with two half-hitches."

He stopped this description of his discovery, for a moment, to steer our pony and our gig elegantly through a narrow bend, while I ventured to ask:

"I assume that these are particular types of knots".

"Just so, Watson, they are sailors' knots. There are a great many knots used in life at sea, for the most diverse purposes. The clove hitch is for example often used to secure a boat, or a ship, to a pile or a bollard; the round turn is used when, in place of a bollard or pile, only a ring in the harbour wall is available. "

"I am amazed at your knowledge, Holmes," I said, quite truthfully.

Holmes had often told me that a man's brain, in his view, is like a little empty attic, with limited space, to be stocked with such furniture as one may choose. That he had such a knowledge of maritime knots was therefore all the more surprising.

"As in this case," he explained, "the knots used to secure someone tell us much about the person who used them. I resolved therefore some time ago to prepare a small monograph on the subject. As I have completed the chapter on seamen's knots, I may at least now use it."

"You are then telling me, if I rightly follow, Holmes, that the person who brought Mr. Pascoe to the engine house was connected with the sea."

"Quite so, Watson"

I found this conclusion more confusing than helpful. The idea that a seaman could be the murderer of a rich banker was troubling, because I could see no possible justification for such an act. But before I could express my doubt, Holmes turned to me again and spoke in a voice that allowed no contradiction.

"I will call now at the hotel, Watson, to set you down, and then go to the local police station, to inform them of the grisly discovery we have made. How long that may take, I cannot judge, but in addition, I will look and listen for a while in Liskeard and also send off a telegram. I would suggest, therefore, that you, old friend, do not wait for me, but that you should retire early, rest from your experience, and be ready so that tomorrow morning we may start early to go to Gorran Haven."

He spoke with such energy that I could no longer object, although I would have asked what his next actions might be. I therefore decided to follow his wise advice, and to exercise my patience until a suitable moment would arise.

Holmes sets out the case

It will however scarcely surprise you, dear reader, to learn that I found little sleep in this night. Holmes was, as he had said, there next morning, and I could not tell whether he had in the night even been to bed. I knew all too well how his energy and restlessness drove him to abuse his constitution, all the more when his hunting instinct told him he was on a promising trail. So it was now, for I found him at breakfast radiant with enthusiasm and energy, while I probably looked as exhausted as I now felt.

There had been at first no opportunity to speak privately with him, but as soon as we were settled in a first class compartment of the Great Western Railway, and as we set off westwards again, I resolved to ask him about his investigations in Liskeard, and about our next steps. This time he did not hesitate to recount his experiences.

"First of all I went to the telegraph office, in order to tell Lord Robartes of the death of Mr. Pascoe, and to ask his help in reaching Gorran Haven with all speed. There followed, as I told you last night, a visit to the police station. The officer receiving me took down my statement, thanked me for my concern, and released me with the reassurance that the matter would now be in the hands of the police, and that

I should not concern myself further. My address at Lanhydrock and in our good old Baker Street, should they later require any further statement, seemed not to be of great concern. Indeed, I found the doubtful opinion, which Lord Robartes had already expressed about these guardians of public order, to be equally justified here; I fear we need have no great expectations for a solution to the murder of Mr. Pascoe. They will surely seek the culprit among the usual suspects, the tramps and vagabonds, of the district. Then, in due course and after a respectful delay, I suspect that they will give up the case."

Holmes' bitterness in respect of the expected inadequacy of the police investigations, both in general and in this district in particular, was not to be missed.

"Then you will presumably now continue to investigate, on your own, whatever may shed light upon this murder."

"Exactly, Watson. And it proves to be all the more necessary, since the murder of Mr. Pascoe clearly stands in a direct connection with the list that Mr. Reeve once had in his notebook."

Surprised, I looked at Holmes, as he leaned back, closed his eyes and put his fingers together. Then he started with the following explanation: "When I left you, yesterday afternoon, in the care of the farmer's wife, I went with her husband to examine again the engine house, where we had found the body. I asked him whether many strangers came up there to Minions, now, and he confirmed my expectation, that since the mines had closed this was not the case. Only occasional visitors came up, now and again, to see the Hurlers and the Cheesewring. Then I asked him whether he had perhaps seen such visitors on Friday the fifth of September for, as you recall, Watson, that was the day that Mr. Pascoe left his house in Lostwithiel and failed to arrive in Liskeard. It appears that the concept of time for the rural population is in a different dimension, compared to city dwellers with their diaries, for this good man took some time to place it, not without difficulties, until he remembered that one of his sheep had an injury, and he that had had to carry it down to the farm. He had then seen, at the side of the road, a cart, with two horses, and a little time later saw two men, who had obviously been up to the stone circles, and were now returning to the cart. One of them walked purposefully, but the other was unsteady. I asked if he could better describe them, and although, as he said, he was too far away to see clearly, he could not forget the conspicuous red hair of the man walking in front, for even in the evening light it seemed copper-coloured."

Holmes paused for a moment, and awaited my conclusion.

"Then, if I understand, Holmes, your opinion is that Ian Reeve, the dismissed clerk of the lawyer's practice in Fowey, helped an unknown man to bring Mr. Pascoe to Minions. They used the cart that the farmer had seen. As soon as they had left Mr. Pascoe, bound and made fast, to his fate in the engine house, they left Minions and the moor. But they had both been seen by the farmer."

Holmes nodded in acknowledgment as I spoke. As I finished, however, he spoke again:

"Excellent, Watson. But in one point you are in error. The man whom Mr. Reeves accompanied, is no longer unknown to us."

This unexpected information took my words away for a moment. There followed, spurred by curiosity, a torrent of words.

"What in Heaven do you mean, Holmes? Are you telling me that you know the name of this unknown stranger, who answers for the murder of Mr. Pascoe, and who, as you yesterday suggested, is connected with the sea?"

"That is quite right, Watson, and remember that I said 'us,' that is, that you know his name too."

"I most certainly do not," I disclaimed, with as much conviction as I felt.

"I think it might come to you, Watson, when I tell you more of what I learned in Liskeard yesterday evening. And you will perhaps recall the sketch map which you had drawn."

I would surely have preferred that Holmes told me the name outright, but if I had tried to force his hand, I knew he might well just stop and leave me knowing no more until the whole matter was clear. I prepared, therefore, like it or not, and as so often, to be patient as he gave me the following description: "The fact that Mr. Reeve and your unknown person, let us say for simplicity Mr. X, had used a cart, and that we already knew that such a waggon had been hired in Liskeard, set me off to every stable and hire business in Liskeard to visit. My efforts have certainly left some of my shoe-leather along the way, but in the end I was rewarded. The blacksmith at the east end recalled clearly that an older well-dressed man had hired a cart and two horses, on the fifth of September. Next day the man had brought the horses and cart back, and hired a single riding-horse. He hired it for two days, and in fact only brought it back after a week. But the blacksmith made no complaint about the customer, for he was generously paid. I thanked him for his help, and as I gave him a half-sovereign and was about to leave, as I noticed he was in some way troubled. I found another half-sovereign, and he then told me that just after the older man had taken his horse and set off southwards, another, younger, man came into the smithy, in great haste, and also asked for a riding horse. He was obviously in a hurry, for hardly had they settled the hire, but he jumped in the saddle and set off, also to the south, at the gallop. That was not all, for the young man had cheated him; the horse had, to this day, not been returned. That was undoubtedly a hard loss for the honest blacksmith. To my question concerning the young man, he could only say that although his features said little, he had worn a good suit which had perhaps seen better days, and the only striking feature was his blazing red hair, with the grey stripes through it."

Holmes stopped again, and looked at me expectantly. It was clear that the description was of Mr. Reeve. But how could that in any way reveal the name of the unknown person, Mr X? Rather doubtfully, even helplessly, I looked at my friend, whose face showed his surprise, even irritation, that I was so slow to follow him. That made me all the more uncomfortable that I could not begin to answer him as he intended; and so, finally, I was truly relieved when he turned again to me and, with some resignation, said: "The unknown man is, naturally, Mr Simon Osborn."

I was again confused, and looked again at my friend. I knew that I had heard the name, but what was the context? I searched in my memory. It would have been much easier to look back into my notebook, but now that I was challenged, I felt I had to prove to Holmes that I was really aware of all the circumstances of the case. And then it came to me; Holmes had himself given me the name. Thankful for at least this recall of my memory, I burst out suddenly with "You mean the American, who had mandated Mr. Hoole, the lawyer in Fowey, to give to Mrs. Lang the legacy to which she was due."

"Just so, Watson. That is exactly the one I mean."

Still incredulous, and confused, I looked at him again. What might an American have to do with all that we had learned? It was clear to Holmes from my face that I had no explanation, so he, with no further prompting, came to my help.

"The description offered by the blacksmith in Liskeard, by the owner of the Three Pilchards in Polperro, and by the manager of the King of Prussia Hotel in Fowey, all correspond strikingly. Moreover, Mr. Osborn already knew well the energetic Mr. Reeve, for he had called several times at the hotel to report on his search for Mrs. Lang."

Holmes again paused, and so, in my continuing incredulity, I asked again what it meant.

"Holmes, that the two men were acquainted is clear. And as you say, the descriptions of the unknown person and of Mr. Osborn appear to correspond. What then is not clear to me is why then Mr. Osborn might have any interest in the murder of Mr. Pascoe. But you also included the owner of The Three Pilchards. Would you then imply that old Samuel Snell's fatal fall into the harbour was perhaps not an accident at all?"

Holmes nodded, in agreement, with my words. It appeared that the doubts which I displayed had amused him. But the slight smile disappeared at once, as he began to lay out his explanations, doing so not as if we were in a railway compartment, but back on the sofa in Baker Street.

"My dear friend, I think the time has come to present to you my picture of the case, as I have so far, with all the available indications, been able to reconstitute it. Let us start shortly before Mr. Reeve lost his place in Mr. Hoole's chambers. We will then follow events, at best in chronological order. Mr. Osborn appears completely satisfied with the work of Mr. Reeve, as instructed by Mr. Hoole, and so he asks Mr. Reeve directly, but privately, to secure information on four further persons. These are Willoughby Pascoe, Reginald Dunstan, Jack Tonkin and Samuel Snell. Mr. Reeve noted the names, in his notebook, in which he always recorded his investigations. He carries out the task and can soon complete his notes with a second column, with the whereabouts and the professional positions of these persons. Having done this, Mr. Reeve gives his notes to his client, which explains the missing page in his notebook.

"Whether Mr. Osborn has any further work for Mr Reeve, or whether the latter himself offers his services, after losing his job, I cannot say. We know however from the manager of the King of Prussia in Fowey that Mr. Reeve now comes frequently to visit Mr. Osborn. During these meetings, Mr. Osborn as we may imagine gives his instructions to Mr. Reeve and provides him with money, as it would not otherwise be possible for him, out of work and already in debt, to visit all the places involved. In return, Mr

142

Osborn receives even more information concerning the four persons. I cannot at this moment know whether at that point it was the intention of Mr. Osborn to bring about the death of the four, but at least, at the latest when he charged Mr. Reeve with making the acquaintance of Mr. Pascoe, he was now pursuing this objective.

"The visits to the Fortuna Club were paid for by Mr. Osborn in the hope that, well, putting it discreetly, his by now known preference for young men might lead him to leave with Mr. Reeve for Liskeard. It may be that as Mr. Pascoe offered no resistance by this point, Mr. Reeve had already given him a strong sleeping draft. That would present no difficulty if they had chosen then to wait for the train in the station buffet, and there taken a glass together, in anticipation of the pleasures to come. It might also have been so, that they used chloroform to render Mr. Pascoe unconscious on his arrival. He could then have been readily lifted into the cart, which Mr. Osborn had hired, and then taken, inconspicuously, to Minions, a lonely but readily accessible place, which Mr. Reeves would have known. Mr. Osborn and Mr. Reeve laid the still unconscious Mr. Pascoe, tied and bound, in the corner of the engine house and left him there.

"I suspect that it was at this point that Mr. Reeve started to take account of what he had now undertaken. That would certainly account for his behaviour with the blacksmith in Liskeard. If you will now look at the sketch map which you had drawn, as I suggested, you will see that Polperro is just in that direction which Mr. Osborn took, followed by Mr. Reeve. The landlord of the Three Pilchards remembered very well the generous old stranger who took good care that old Samuel Snell drank much more than was good for him. It would have been an easy matter for Mr. Osborn, who left the house before closing time, to entangle Mr. Snell in the nets lying around and to roll him, weighted with a small anchor, into the harbour.

"Less satisfying would have been his encounter with Mr. Reeve, who had followed him to Polperro and had, I suspect, seen the murder of Samuel Snell. Should this really have been the case, then we might reflect that Mr. Osborn is described by all as an older, unhealthy looking man, while Mr. Reeve is a young man. I fear that rather than preventing the murder, which he might have done, he had seen the opportunity to blackmail Mr. Osborn. This, if it were so, might have had the result of which we learned earlier from Mr. Tremayne in Lanhydrock, that his lifeless body fell out of a barrel of pilchards being unloaded in Mevagissey. You see therefore Watson that in my view the murder of Mr. Reeve is also to be charged to Mr. Osborn's account. The suggestion that his gambling friends might have murdered him seemed to me even at the time to be misplaced."

I asked Holmes at this point, as he paused, why he felt so categorically that that was so.

"Well, now, Watson, a first and plausible reason is that dead men most surely do not repay their debts. A second reason is that if one of these persons really had killed Mr. Reeve, so as to make of him a warning example to others, it would then be natural that the punishment attract as much attention as possible. A corpse concealed in a fish barrel will not achieve that. But let us now think about Mr. Osborn. If he had had a fight with a younger man, it would surely have taxed him severely. That may explain why he spent longer around Polperro, to recover his strength, and could only then return the horse, a week later than agreed, to the blacksmith's yard in Liskeard.

The other matter to consider is the death of Mr. Reginald Dunstan, a quiet and withdrawn merchant, with heart trouble, living in St. Austell. To this I can only offer a hypothesis, because, as we know, all that we have is from hearsay. Perhaps his death was indeed natural; but it might equally be that Mr. Osborn visited him, and perhaps poisoned him, or that he so threatened him, so that his heart failed of fear or shock. But now there is only one more person on the list, and that is why we are now on the way to Gorran Haven. The way there from St. Austell is long and laborious, especially for a person who is elderly and ill. I suspect therefore that our murder must have taken time to rest, before he strikes again. Should my suspicion be correct, we may just be in time not only to save the life of Mr Tonkin, but we should also be in a position to learn what it is that moved Mr. Osborn to commit these crimes. Believe me, Watson, I am convinced that the reason for these murders lies somewhere in the past. We know that two of the victims had been actively involved in smuggling, Samuel Snell probably with unloading and hiding the boxes and barrels of the cargo, while Reginald Dunstan would have been the one who organised the transport and the sale of the goods.

"Now then, Watson, what else would it need, to sustain such smuggling operations?"

I shrugged my shoulders in ignorance, but Holmes went on.

"It needs someone who can purchase the goods to be smuggled, and can supply a ship, and a trusted captain and crew. That means a person with adequate financial means, in the background. That person was the old Mr. Pascoe and, indirectly, his son Willoughby. So we see that already three of the names on the list are tied together. But let us not forget, that this is still only one hypothesis, which I offer as corresponding to the facts so far known to us. We may find the truth when we talk with Mr. Tonkin, and when we can apprehend the murderer."

Here Holmes stopped, and there was for a few moments a tense silence in our compartment. A shrill whistle outside, from the locomotive, surprised me all the more, breaking the silence. Holmes looked at his pocket-watch and, almost absent-mindedly, said: "We are almost at the station for St. Austell."

The train slowed down, and I saw waiting passengers on the platform. Holmes was already standing. Before I did the same, I asked him outright a question which followed from all he had told me, and which now left me unable to find my peace.

"And what then, if we arrive too late and find Mr. Tonkin no longer alive?"

"Then, Watson, Mr. Osborn has won the game, and we will no longer be able to learn the truth. The secret which binds Mr. Osborn and these persons on the list would then remain buried in their past," replied Holmes, in a voice which betrayed some bitterness.

With this he opened the compartment door, and turned to me to add lightly, but with a somewhat melancholy smile,

"My friend, how did Wolfgang von Goethe express it so succinctly in 'Faust'? The past is a book with seven seals'."

Gorran Haven

Scarcely had we left the train, than I discovered Mr. Jenkins, the Steward of Lanhydrock, approaching with rapid steps.

"Mr. Holmes, Dr. Watson, please follow me, His Lordship has instructed me to bring you as quickly as I can to the loading station of the Pentewan Railway on the West Road. I have hired a gig, which is waiting here for you."

With these words Mr. Jenkins turned and walked briskly to the back of the station building. Holmes and I followed his example, so that within minutes we were all three sitting in this small, but lively, vehicle. Mr. Jenkins led us skilfully through the narrow alleys and streets, which were most confusing to me, and seemed always to change their orientation. I had lost completely my sense of direction, when we emerged on an open yard, where several horses and carts, heavily loaded with sacks, were waiting. Mr. Jenkins had explained as we rode with him that the Pentewan Railway had once been built as a horse tramway, to carry the China clay of the St. Austell district down to ships in the harbour of Pentewan. Once upon a time the neighbouring harbour of Charleston, further east, with its two dock basins, had hoped to have the tramway, but Pentewan had been chosen, not least because of the easier access. It was possible on the upper part of the tramway, with its descending grade, to allow the loaded clay wagons to roll, practically under their own weight, downhill. On the lower part of the line, horses were at first used, and these also brought the empty wagons back to St. Austell.

Fifteen years ago the rails had been strengthened, and now steam locomotives could be used. Despite this, the Pentewan Railway suffered financial losses, because in the middle of the eighteen seventies the Great Western Railway, with the Cornwall Railway, had also obtained a railway connection to Fowey, over which the China clay transport from the whole district was more effective. His last remark was that the transport volumes had just in the last four years started slowly to recover.

He stopped the pony, and swung lightly out of his seat. Walking briskly to speak with the locomotive driver, Mr. Jenkins turned round to us as we approached. He smiled to say that all was clear, and explained, obviously rather relieved: "Yes, gentlemen, all in in order, you are to ride on the locomotive". My face must have betrayed my surprise, for Mr. Jenkins quickly continued: "You will remember, gentlemen, that the Pentewan Railway was never equipped for passengers, although it happens from time to time. Passengers are then carried in the clay wagons. Lord Robartes used his contacts to ensure that you can, at short notice, use the line, and also that the locomotive will make a special trip, without wagons, which will materially reduce the journey time. So I wish you a good trip."

We expressed our thanks, and, taking our leave of Mr. Jenkins set about climbing onto this small steam engine, which, I saw, carried the name 'Trewithan'. The strong arm of the fireman and the warm welcome of the driver helped me on board, and I heard Holmes ask the steward what would follow: "And how do we continue from Pentewan, Mr. Jenkins?"

"Oh, forgive me, Mr. Holmes, I had not described the continuation, but all is taken care of. In the harbour Captain Brooke will be waiting for you with the steam launch Veritas. This vessel belongs to a judge in Truro who, at his Lordship's request, has kindly put it at your disposal."

"Thank you very much, Mr. Jenkins – and please thank Lord Robartes for all his help," replied Holmes, and climbed, much more elegantly than I had done a moment before, up to the footplate of the 'Trewithan'. I will not burden your patience, dear reader, with an all-too-detailed description of this trip on a steam locomotive on a narrow-gauge railway. Allow me however to say that it was much noisier, dirtier and more uncomfortable than I had ever imagined. I could not recall in my whole life being so completely shaken as during this journey. And yet it was an experience I would not in any circumstance have missed. The dream, which every young boy has, to ride on a locomotive, had for me become reality.

In the harbour in Pentewan we found Captain Brooke waiting for us, to bring us to the Veritas, which already had steam up and was ready to put to sea at once. As I sought out the small cabin, with Holmes, I was pleased to find a seat, for my endeavours to keep my balance on the locomotive had again caused my leg to suffer. Now, however, there was another concern. The weather began to deteriorate, and the brisk wind which we had already experienced in the early morning in Liskeard stiffened noticeably. The further we followed the coast, the worse it became. The grey clouds were now darker, and built themselves up, before the wind, into threatening forms. Our steam launch remained as close to the shore as was wise, but it was tossed back and forth by the rising waves of a rough sea. The moment came, where my stomach capitulated before this rolling and pitching. I had no choice but to seek a place on deck, at the rail, from which I could pay my tribute to King Neptune. I therefore beg the reader to forgive me, that my recollections of this voyage, along a beautiful coastline and past the fishing port of Mevagissey, are regrettably rudimentary.

It was already late afternoon as we reached the harbour mouth at Gorran Haven with its more sheltered calm. This is a natural small bay with a sandy beach. The tide allowed that we entered and took our place behind the harbour wall, a stone-built quay wall, behind which the fishing boats find moorings sheltered from the storms at sea. The many fishing boats which were now, as we with our steam launch did, seeking protection, suggested that this was the principal occupation of the residents of Gorran Haven. As we passed the end of the quay, it appeared that part of the wall had been newly built. The older parts still visible left me with the impression that Gorran Haven had been for centuries a fishing village. In the village itself, we saw houses built in grey granite, nestling close together in the steep street, and the impression, despite here and there a whitewashed cottage, was at first dark and threatening,

As soon as Captain Brooke had found his mooring and made fast, Holmes and I went ashore, leaving behind our travelling bags, while Captain Brooke saw to the boat, on which he would await us next morning. Around the harbour all seemed deserted. Clearly the population had taken refuge from the now darkly threatening storm in good time. No-one was near, who might direct us to the Anchor Inn. A wind-driven drizzle was now setting in. I looked questioningly at Holmes, who pointed up to the village, and set off. As I followed, I saw his searching gaze alight on a tower, threatening at first sight, just above us, which, as we climbed the hill, turned out to be the tower of St. Just church, set like a watchtower over the harbour. Where there was a church, there was surely a vicarage, and a helpful soul who might direct us on our way. Following my friend, I fought against the wind to the church gate.

We knocked vigorously at the vicarage door, three times on the heavy iron knocker, and it suddenly swung open. There stood before us a homely, solid-looking man, whom I estimated to be in his early thirties. Before we could speak, he led us inside, with the warm words, "Come inside, gentlemen, come in quickly, this is no time to stand talking in the street!" We entered a hallway and then, as he took our wet cloaks, into a room warmed by a roaring fire in the fireplace. Here were two comfortable armchairs, in which he kindly invited us to take our place. This room was the vicar's study, and he introduced himself as the Reverend Henry Gibbs, offering us with friendly words not only a warm chair, but a brandy. I sensed that Holmes, possessed as he was with our hunt for Tonkin, was impatient, and, but I, still weak from the voyage, accepted this generous gesture, while the gracious clergyman brought a stool and addressed us. "And now, my dear sirs, you may tell me who you are."

"My name is Sherlock Holmes and this is my good friend Dr. Watson", answered Holmes.

"I am pleased to make your acquaintance, gentlemen, the more so as it seems you are not from this lonely corner, this remote wasteland to which my bishop has dispatched me. Am I right?"

This good man looked at us with interest, and, as Holmes appeared lost in thought as he stared into the fire, I resolved to answer. "Quite so, Reverend Gibbs. We are presently guests of Lord Robartes at Lanhydrock, but we come from London, where I have a doctor's practice, and …", but I came no further as Holmes suddenly interrupted. "We are taking a holiday as his guests, and were discovering the region. Friends had told us on no account to miss Gorran

Haven, and while there, to call in at the Anchor Inn. Could you perhaps tell us how we might get there?"

Rev. Gibbs looked at us in what was clearly complete surprise. He seemed to search for words, and it was a moment before he could answer Holmes. "Well, yes, Mr. Holmes. The Anchor is some distance away from the village. It is up the hill, following the path that leads around the cliff, and on towards Dodman Point. You will not miss it, when you go back down this street to the harbour, keep left and then take the first path on the right, which climbs steeply uphill. You will come onto a firmly trodden ancient path, the so-called old coastal path. This runs along the whole of the coast, and was used by the Coastguards, as they tried to frustrate the evil business of the smugglers and wreckers. But permit me, gentlemen, to say that with the best will I can hardly imagine that you were recommended to the Anchor Inn"

"And why is that?" I asked.

"Well, firstly, because the Anchor is not at all a respectable inn, but simply a run-down retreat for our worst drinkers. And secondly, because the landlord is a notoriously violent and godless character. The Anchor is surely not the proper address for two gentlemen like yourselves."

"You make a severe judgment upon Mr. Tonkin, Reverend. Have you known him long?" asked Holmes.

"No, Mr. Holmes, I have not known him long, but meeting him was enough to remain with me as a most unpleasant recollection. I have been performing my duties in Gorran Haven now for some two years. I have seen most of my parishioners, when not every Sunday in church, at least at Christmas or at Easter. Jack Tonkin was not one of them. I therefore decided, one day, to visit him at the Inn, and to share with him the Word of God. Old Tonkin reacted promptly; he pulled a weapon out from under the bar, and fired a shot into the table beside me. I admit that I wasted no time in further deliberation, but quickly put a safe distance between us."

"Does Mr. Tonkin treat all his guests so aggressively?" asked Holmes.

"That I cannot say, Mr. Holmes. The older village people have told me that when he was a young man, Jack Tonkin had a terrible reputation. As were many here, in the village, he was not only a fisherman, but also a smuggler and a wrecker. But then, quite suddenly, almost overnight he built the house in the hill, the Anchor Inn, and opened for business. Hearsay has it however, that it was, from its opening, first and foremost a meeting point for the smugglers and their cargoes. But the smuggling had passed its peak, and as there were no more rich profits to be made, the Anchor lost its trade. It has, as I learned, been an open secret for years, that as far as the consumption of strong drinks goes, old Tonkin has been his own best customer."

"Thank you for your hospitality, Rev. Gibbs. Forgive me, but it really is time that we are on our way. I would greatly like to see this Mr. Tonkin face to face. He will surely be up there?" said Holmes and rose to his feet.

Resigned to the realisation that he had not discouraged us from our planned visit to the Anchor Inn, the vicar answered, "You will certainly find him at this time at his Inn. He never leaves the village. This morning I saw him in the village buying fresh fish. Should he suggest that you dine with him, I suggest you refuse. Word has it, that his skills as a cook are no better than his behaviour."

With this, the kindly vicar, having loaned us two lanterns, escorted us, with our cloaks, to the door. We headed off again into the wind.

Times long past

The last part of the path leading to the Anchor Inn led along a narrow way. We were now above the cliffs which here fell steeply to the sea. We were completely exposed to the fierceness of the elements, and violent gusts forced us several times to stop and await a calm moment. Even so, it was not always easy to stop; the wind tore in all directions, and even keeping our feet was not easy. The reader will therefore imagine how relieved I was, as we reached the Inn. The door was closed, but a faint light escaped the closed window shutters. I imagined that Mr Tonkin, with long experience, had like many of his Gorran Haven neighbours barricaded himself inside his house against the approaching storm. Holmes and I took our sticks and both hammered together on the door, but at first there was no response. Had we failed to overcome the noise of the storm? No, at last the door opened and an elderly man appeared in the doorway, who stared at us with a confused expression. Holmes said nothing, so I attempted to address him, shouting to overcome the howling wind.

"Mr. Tonkin, can we come in? ... It is most important that we speak with you."

The figure in the doorway did not reply, and looked at us apparently without understanding. I hoped that our conversation with Mr Tonkin was not to end at this point, for the rain, which had started again, now drove in over us with redoubled force. Behind us we heard approaching rolls of thunder. It was very clear, that at any moment the heavens would open over us all. But Holmes, alongside me, suddenly broke into my thoughts with a rapid movement. He had drawn the dagger out of his walking stick and held it now to the chest of our silent partner. I looked sharply from Tonkin to Holmes, as he cried out triumphantly, with a voice that seemed to echo even over the thunder: "Watson, you are mistaken. This man is not the landlord, but Mr. Osborn."

Completely surprised, I looked at Holmes, whose vigilant eyes never moved from our opposite number. Then he spoke again, sharply and with a force which I had seldom heard.

"We will go inside. We will all go into the house. You, Mr Osborn, go first. Halt! ... Sit down at the first table. Good ... and now lay your hands on the table."

While Holmes was speaking, he followed with the dagger every move of Mr. Osborn. Once inside, I closed the door of the Inn behind me and stood at the side of my friend.

I was thus ready to intervene, should need arise, without inhibiting his own radius of action. Holmes now spoke again with authority to our prisoner. "You are indeed a most dangerous man, Mr. Osborn. Or should I rather say Mr. Oakley to you? As so many do, who change their names, you preferred to keep your old initials. Out of Silas Oakley there emerged Simon Osborn."

Confused, I looked again at Holme. Silas Oakley? I knew that I had already heard the name, but where? And what was the connection? But before I could place it, Holmes came with the explanation, and brought my memory back.

"Watson, this man here is the brother of Mrs. Lang. She believed him lost at sea. He has returned after many years, to bring his sister a legacy and to commit murder. Then Holmes turned back to Osborn and said: "You at first were helped by Ian Reeve of the lawyer's practice in Fowey, until he became a burden to you. You have made a systematic search for four men, and I know that at least three of them are no longer alive. So I ask you now: where is the owner of this house? What have you done with Mr. Jack Tonkin?"

The eyes of our prisoner, as they watched Holmes, were at first full of hate; and yet, as Holmes made this explanation, his expression turned to one of complete astonishment. It was only some moments after Holmes had completed his allegations that Osborn dropped into an apathetic expression and started to speak, with a monotonous voice.

"What you are telling me, mister, is correct. But I would still like it better if you could call me Osborn. And now, if you want to know about old Jack, just go yourself to the bigger cabinet, in the passage behind the bar. In the floor there is a trapdoor. Open it, and you will see a ladder down into a cellar. The evil villain you are looking for is down there, stone dead."

He stopped speaking and looked defiantly at Holmes.

"Watson, would you look and see if he is speaking the truth? But be very careful."

Hardly had he spoken, than I was on my feet, to do as my friend had wished. In the passage there was a lantern, which I took with me.

Returning shortly afterwards to the bar-room, I could only confirm what our prisoner had said. The dead man whom I had found had, apart from scratches in the face and on his knuckles, no visible injuries. The cause of death was a broken neck. Whether this resulted from a fight or a fall would be difficult to determine. Grimly, Holmes looked searchingly at the prisoner, as he said: "Mr. Osborn, you have achieved your aim. I do not know whether this pleases you or not, but I can assure you that any satisfaction will be of a short duration. I can promise you that in this whole affair Her Majesty's hangman will very soon have the last word."

Holmes understood the effect his words were having. The already pale complexion which marked our prisoner had now become almost waxen, as if already of a dead man. He spoke again in his monotonous voice:

"I'm not afraid of dying. Death I need not fear, for I have seen it too often. And even without your hangman, I have little enough time left. … But I would have liked to have had this little time in freedom."

"You might have thought of that before you laid hand on your victims," I broke out angrily.

Our prisoner screwed up his eyes and looked at me in anger, and then fell back into a fit of wild laughter. He took some moments to recover and then said, with a chilling contempt in his voice,

"Victims! … Those were no victims. They were all evildoers, wicked, all of them, only Reeve not, but he was only after my money."

There followed a moment of silence, and then Holmes turned again to our prisoner.

"Mr. Osborn, as I have already told you, I know what you have done. With the help of various witnesses who have seen you and who will be called upon to testify, the jury in court will have no problem in establishing your guilt. Perhaps your time in prison might pass more comfortably, if you show yourself prepared to help me."

Here Holmes allowed a short pause, while he looked searchingly at the prisoner, so that the latter asked suspiciously: "What do you want from me?"

"I want to know what this is about. I want to know why."

"That's all a long time ago, mister."

"We are in no hurry", replied Holmes.

Osborn shrugged his shoulders and answered softly:

"Why not? But I'd be happier if you would stop threatening me all the time with that blade."

Holmes nodded briefly, moved to the side of the table, and put the dagger on the bar, where it was ready to be seized at once if called for. I sat opposite, on the other side, careful however to maintain a proper distance from Mr.

Osborn. I then took my notebook, in which I recorded the following account as it was told to us by Osborn himself.

"I was born in Gorran Haven. My father was a poor fisherman, without his own boat. His life was bitterly hard, and all the harder for an accident which took away the use of his left hand. No-one had work for a cripple. But the smugglers knew, and they could use him. At first he helped with the unloading of the boats, because his back was still broad and strong, and he could shift a heavy load. Sometimes he was the look-out."

I looked up puzzled, and Holmes explained: "Mr. Osborn will have us know that his father was on watch, to warn his smuggler friends, if there were any danger of a coastguards' patrol."

I nodded in reply, to this explanation, and returned to my notebook. Holmes prompted Mr. Osborn to continue: "Please carry on, Mr. Osborn."

"I helped my father, whenever I could, even as a child. In our band, with the others, there were Samuel Snell and Jack Tonkin. Our job was to hide the smuggled goods in the caves by the beach. From there they would be shared out with others, who would sell them for us. That's how I came to know Reginald Dunstan. He was a storeman for a mining company and so he could sell the smuggled wares, on the side, to the miners. But the head of the band was old Pascoe, with his terrible son."

Here Mr. Osborn broke off his story, and asked if he might have a glass of brandy. Talking, he added, made him thirsty. And with a suggestive glance he said there was more than enough to drink here in the Inn. I looked to Holmes, who nodded his agreement, stood up and brought a brandy to satisfy our prisoner's wish. It had caught my notice that Mr. Osborn suffered from excessive salivation, and the spirits might give him some relief. Even so, he continued to lift a large handkerchief to his mouth. With surprise, I saw that his mouth and gums were also bleeding. Despite this, he continued with his account.

"With his own money, the older Pascoe underwrote our smuggling band. He arranged for the goods to be bought in France, and he chartered the ship and the crew for the voyage. His son took over the work at this end. He watched that the captain and crew kept to their word, and saw to it that the unloading and hiding of the contraband were carried out as agreed. Often he cheated the men of their agreed share.

But with his rich and influential father in the background, nobody dared to cause trouble.

"Willoughby Pascoe became ever more brutal. He seemed to delight in humiliating people, and to torment them. And that's where the story takes its turn. On an August night in 1844, when I was just 12 years old, I was helping to stow the smuggled wares in our cave. Suddenly young Willoughby was at my side and dragging me into the inner cave. He stroked my cheek, saying what a handsome boy I was. I had no idea what he was up to, but it was unpleasant, and I tried to break away. But his fingers gripped my arm, and he pressed me closer, reached into my hair, pulled my head back and tried to kiss me. His panting hot breath seemed to hit me in the face. I screamed with all my might.

"All of a sudden his grasp, which had pinned me down, gave way – I was free. I jumped up and ran as fast as my legs would carry me, towards the larger cave, but almost ran into Jack, Reginald and Samuel, who must have come to see what was going on. Only then could I pause to see what had saved me. It was my father, who shouted, "Get your hands off my boy," and had in fury already landed a few hard blows on Willoughby, who was on the floor, his lip and nose bleeding. My father broke off, turned to me and took me by the hand to take me home. Behind us, as we left the cave, I heard Willoughby ranting and swearing, "I'll get you, you'll pay for this, you dog." But that was, as I later heard, not the last shock for Willoughby on that unforgettable night.

"My father took me home, so no one was watching out, and a little later came disaster: Willoughby and the three others were discovered by a patrolling coastguard. They gave him short shrift, like others before him. He died quickly, stabbed with a fish knife. But this time, instead of disposing of his body by the cliffs, Willoughby saw a chance to get his own back. They carried the coastguard's body to the coastal path, and left the fish knife nearby. It was my father's knife, with his name burned into the handle, and he had lost it from his belt in the fight. My father's fate was sealed; he was arrested next day, imprisoned and soon faced a court, with a jury which could do no other than find him guilty. But everyone knew that I was, for my father, in all things his 'left hand,' and they decided I must have been there with him as the coastguard was killed. So they came for me, and Jack Tonkin was ready to swear that I had boasted, in his hearing, that I had helped in the murder. So I was convicted as well.

"My father was sentenced to death by hanging, and me? I got 'life.' But just then the prisons were grossly overfilled, and the court decided that I should be transported, sent to one of the overseas prison colonies. Until my father died, they kept me in Bodmin Jail. That was an evil place, all dark passages, filthy and stinking, and I never forgot it. Nor can I forget the cries and moaning of the other prisoners. And on the day they hanged my father, they took me to Plymouth, to put me on a prison ship bound for Van Diemen's Land."

"Van Diemen's Land?" I repeated, interrupting Osborn. A little irritated, Holmes explained: "That was the name by which present-day Tasmania was known. The name was that of a former governor-general of the Dutch East Indies, who first commissioned a voyage of exploration along the Australian south coast. Abel Tasman, a Dutch sea captain, undertook this expedition. He discovered not only New Zealand, but also this big island, although he at first thought it to be a peninsular on the Australian mainland. It was only in 1798 that a British Captain, Matthew Flinders, discovered the Bass Strait, and demonstrated that Van Diemen's Land is an island. In 1856 the island was renamed, in honour of its first discoverer." I nodded my understanding to Holmes, and waited for Mr. Osborn to continue his account.

"I cannot begin to say how terrible this sea voyage was. The lack of fresh air and space, and the dreadful food, made most of us ill, and a lot died on the way. As we reached Van Diemen's Land we were first put in a camp, and then shared out among various farms. I worked for half a year, and got to know Will Pearce, who had already made two escape attempts. He was about to try again, and I offered, indeed, I begged to go with him. He was an experienced sailor, and knew that someone like me, with some knowledge of the sea might be a help when he was on the run. So he took me with him, although I was only a lad, and might also be a burden to him.

"There were twelve of us who overcame the overseer and broke out that night. We stole a boat in a small harbour, and made it to Hobart Town, the capital of Van Diemen's Land. Then we split up, because a big group was too obvious. Will Pearce and I, we hired on a sailing ship which was carrying a cargo of barrels of whale oil to Chile. We made it, and there Will and I went separate ways and I found a station as a lad sailor on a ship which would bring me to Mexico, and then to North America. That was a long, hard voyage, with many perils and privations, and sometimes I wondered if it might not have been better to stay in the prison colony. But we reached the west coast of North America, and I put my feet on land and knew that now I was at last a free man, and all my doubts were behind me."

Mr. Osborn made a pause, and took another brandy. Holmes appeared to be following Osborn's account dispassionately, but I had to admit that the history, which our prisoner recounted, moved me greatly. However much I deplored the evildoing which Osborn had already admitted, I felt a deep sympathy for that poor boy of so many years ago. But there was no time to dwell on it now, for he was speaking again.

"In California I found my way to Sacramento, and I lived from underpaid odd jobs and pickpocketing. That was how I got to know Mr Sutter, because I tried to steal his pocketbook. But he didn't take me to the sheriff; he took me with him to New Helvetia in the Sacramento Valley. This was a farm colony which he had himself founded, and the curious name was because he originally hailed from Switzerland. He had become successful. New Helvetia was fertile, growing, and making a decent profit. He taught me reading and writing, and arithmetic, and I often asked myself why he was so good to me.

"Perhaps it was because when he left home, he already had a shameful history. He had left his creditors in Switzerland and paid his expedition to Sacramento with various swindles – be that as it may, that was a good time for me, in New Helvetia. Sadly, it didn't last long. One of Sutter's foremen, as he was building a sawmill, discovered a gold nugget. That was the start of the Gold Rush, which overran California. The gold-diggers came in thousands, from all over, took Sutter's land and plundered his farm. His workers abandoned him and joined the gold-diggers, so that his harvest failed and his cattle died off. California was only newly part of the United States, and Mr. Sutter could not expect government help to protect his property. It was obvious that New Helvetia was finished. I took my leave of him, and went into the hills, where the gold was mainly to be found, to see what I could find.

It took some time before I had any success. The claim was not rich, and the work very hard. Life in the wooded mountains was often lonely, and it was good to go down to the town to buy food and tools, and to enjoy the saloon with its whisky and girls. It didn't take long to catch on that the prices were higher every time I went, and it seemed to me that everybody was getting rich from the gold, except for the poor miners who dug it up. That was when I decided that when I next had a good find, I would bring it to the bank and that would then be my reserve. With the rest I built a solid cabin on my claim, and that became my home. I lived there mainly from hunting and fishing, until President Abraham Lincoln in 1863, during the Civil War, announced the concessions for building the new Transcontinental Railroad. As quickly as I could, I signed on with the Central Pacific Railroad, which was to build eastwards through the mountains from California. We were to be paid by the number of miles we built, so there were some curious alignments, and of course we were always competing with the Union Pacific who were building from the East. I was strong, and quickly became a foreman with my own team, many of whom were Chinese. The newspapers said there were more than 15,000 Chinese building the line over the Sierra Nevada Mountains. Ah, that was truly a good time. And it was a great feeling, to be there when the two separate rail lines met at Promontory, Utah, above the Great Salt Lake, and on the 10th of May 1869, they had a celebration to drive in the last spike to join them up.

I stayed for a while with the railroad, but I felt myself drawn back again to my mountain home by the river Not much remained, naturally, after several years away, and I set about rebuilding. It wasn't quite so lonely as before, when I had first lived there. There were a few prospectors upstream, but now the gold was mostly excavated by companies which could exploit poor seams, and still find enough to make profits. I had to go further afield, if I wanted to find loneliness and quiet for my hunting. And there came gradually the realisation that I could feel my age, and the hunting trips in the wilderness got less frequent. Hearing and sight were getting weaker, and I thought it was age, but then I noticed that balance and walking were also difficult. Sometimes I staggered and could hardly steer a straight course. And then there was this saliva, and the bleeding gums."

Our prisoner made here another pause, and drank another draught of his brandy. As he did so, I recalled a report that I had recently read in a medical journal. Judging by the symptoms that Mr. Osborn displayed, it seemed clear that he was suffering from severe mercury poisoning. I could imagine that the mercury had entered his body when it was earlier used by the miners, extracting and refining gold, and then also in the contaminated spring water, which he had drunk thinking it was still fresh. I could not pursue my medical judgment, however, because he then again took up his narrative.

"That was when I resolved to ride into town and consult a doctor. He had any number of diplomas on the wall, but he couldn't help. He only said I should visit one of the specialists in a big city. Well, I had always wanted to ride the railroad we had built, and I had money enough. For all events I took some bags of my gold with me. I bought two suits, and everything I thought a traveller should take, and set course for New York. It was a breath-taking journey, but I found myself also thinking of all those emigrants who, caught by the draw of gold, had set out from the East Coast for California, long before there was a railroad. The specialist who took me told me straight, after a long examination, that I had not long to live. Somehow I had already come to that idea. But now the question lay before me, what should I now do with the time remaining to me? How should I use my dwindling strength? Should I go back to my cabin, where I would one day lie helpless until I died, among the lonely hills? But why should I stay here in New York, where I was just as much alone, until death caught up with me?

Nothing seemed right, so it didn't help me, but then came a thought, which was perhaps awakened when I felt again the nearness of the sea. Why shouldn't I go back to my old home in Cornwall? The thought appealed to me and I took the first ship I could find, bound for Plymouth. It was only during the long crossing that I thought that I could try to find my sister Ruth, if she still lived. In the first years after my deportation, I had often thought of my mother and Ruth, but as the years went by I had put those thoughts behind me. But now, face to face with death, I wanted to know what had become of them. Should Ruth still be alive, I did not intend to visit her. Why should I? I would be a complete stranger to her, and I had too little time in prospect to change that. Then I had the thought that the gold, which I was carrying around with me, might find a good home with her and be put to good purpose.

All I knew of my sister was that she was born in Gorran Haven, and probably went with my mother to the poor house in Bodmin. That suggested I should go down further west. Then I had the idea to see what became of the old smuggler band. I remembered that Samuel Snell's brother was a boat-builder in Polperro, and had had a family. If he was alive I might find more out about the old ones. Fowey seemed a good place, where I could start to make enquiries. First I looked for a lawyer, and asked at the Chambers of Mr. Hoole. I left with him a casket, in his care, with the instruction to give it to Ruth Oakley if he could find her. Mr. Reeve, the lawyer's clerk, was entrusted with the search. He made regular reports and did the job so well that I decided, while he was finding my sister, to find out all there was to know about Willoughby Pascoe, Samuel Snell, Jack Tonkin and Reginald Dunstan. For a start I told him all I remembered from the old days. That was obviously enough, as he was at once successful, and he gave me a page of his notebook saying where they were and what they were doing. In the meantime he had found my sister still alive and married, and I was a happy man when I finally learned that she had received the casket with the gold. But then I started to think about the others. Then my anger rose, to think that Reginald, Samuel und Jack had all three let their silence, their lies and perjury be paid for by old Pascoe. They were all better off, even wealthy, and this was all at the cost of my father, hanged for their lies. My mother and little sister went to the poor house, and I had been banished for life.

So when Reeve came to ask me at my hotel whether he could do any more for me, I took him on gratefully. That's how I learned more about their daily affairs, and I asked Reeve to win Willoughby's confidence and get closer contact with him. From that moment it was easy to get him to Liskeard and then to Minions, which was where his dirty money had come from. Reeve knew the old mines in Minions, and was a great help. I don't know if he knew what I was thinking, or if he thought we would simply give Willoughby the fright of his life. After we had left Minions behind us, he suddenly said he didn't want to do any more for me. That was in order, so I took leave of him in Liskeard, and thought that was the end of it. But then he secretly followed me to Polperro, and saw how I tipped the drunken old Samuel Snell into the harbour and left him to drown. Reeve tried then to blackmail me. I let him think he was safe, and took him with me, saying he could have his money in my room at my lodgings. It was already late at night, and he followed me without suspicion as far as the fish factory. Just as he realised that I wasn't going to pay him, I stabbed him two or three times with my knife and it was all over. I had to avoid attention, and I found at the factory a partly filled fish barrel, tipped him in and quickly fixed down the lid.

The night's work had sapped my strength, and it was another day or two later before I could deal with Reginald. I obtained entry under a pretence, and it was only as we sat in his office that I told him who I really was. The sheer horror on his face was already a satisfaction, but I could not enjoy the feeling for long, for within seconds his lips turned blue, he gasped for breath and he pulled at his shirt collar. Then he fell back, his hands at his side, his eyes went blank and his body dropped forwards over his desk. That was much too quick for my liking, but I was determined that the next one would suffer more.

For that I would need all my strength. So I made my plans carefully, and made a quiet journey to Veryan Bay, where I finalized my plans. I was going to take Jack to our old cave, where we had once hidden our smuggled goods, and there was an underground passage between his public house and our cave, where the lower parts were flooded at high tide. I wanted to leave Jack tied up on the rocks there, and wait until he was horribly drowned. Well, I'm sorry it didn't happen. As I drove him at knife-point to go down to the cellar he tried to get back at me. We fought, and both of us fell down into the cellar. I was knocked out, and as I came round I found I was lying on Jack, who was no longer breathing. Badly shaken, I was just on my way to leave the Inn, but when I opened the door you were standing there in the rain."

Mr. Osborn had finished his account. There was a long silence, while each of us thought about the story we had heard. It was Holmes who, in a studied voice, broke the silence. "Mr Osborn, thank you for all you have told us. You have confirmed my suspicions in all respects, and you have clarified the few remaining questions. I am going to ask you now to write your own statement, in my friend's notebook, admitting what you have done here in Cornwall." Osborn nodded weakly, and as I put the notebook, at an empty page, in front of him, he set out to write his confession. Holmes had surely seen, wisely, that Osborn's desperate medical condition made this step necessary. For me too, I doubted whether he would live long enough to see the inside of a courthouse. As soon as Osborn had finished his short text, and Holmes had read it through and shown that he was satisfied, I took up again my notebook, while Holmes spoke again, with authority, and looking sternly at Osborn.

"Now we must go back to Gorran Haven, where you will be put in safe keeping, until arrangements are made for your arrest. As you are obviously well aware of the hopelessness of your position, I will not march you at knife point down the hill, but only secure your hands. Watson, can you go please to find a suitable rope?"

"Naturally, Holmes," I replied. I looked again in the big cupboard in the passage, as I had already seen there various lines and ropes. With Osborn's hands tied behind him, our little procession set off to leave the Anchor Inn behind us. The storm had passed over, the rain had stopped and the wind was no longer so fierce. Even so, the going was not easy. We had our lanterns, but we came only slowly forwards, as the torrential rain, falling while we were in the Inn, had left the ground muddy and slippery. Even the stony path, earlier an easy path, was now, in the darkness, moss-covered as it was, more than perilous. With his bound hands and erratic gait, our prisoner seemed to manage quite well. Holmes followed close behind, in a safe, fluid step, moving easily and reminding me of nothing as much as a cat. I was however in difficulty; the steep descent on this slippery path was very laborious. The tension in my leg had set up at once those pains, from my former bullet wound, which I knew only too well. I had repeatedly to rest, and take the weight off my leg, and so was more and more left behind by the others.

With my eyes always set on the ground just before my feet, in the darkness, I only vaguely saw what suddenly happened in front of me. Our prisoner had attempted to sidestep a slippery stone slab, had left the path and had stepped sideways onto a steeply falling flank of the hill we were descending. Whether, already walking unsteadily, he then lost his balance, or whether the ground gave way under his weight, or indeed whether he saw a chance to end his troubles there and then, I would never know. All I was sure of was a sudden shout, carried away by the wind, and I looked up to both men. I saw by the lantern light how Osborn fell to the ground, and he slid helplessly towards the cliff. With his bound hands he had no way to help himself. Holmes left the path, and grabbed to try to hold him. To my dread, however, I saw how, in doing so, my friend himself slipped and fell. I heard a long shout, and the light of the lantern disappeared. It was over in seconds. I was holding my breath, my legs weak as if they could never carry me. My throat was choking, my stomach cramped to a painful knot. Then all seemed clear again, and I shouted as loud as I could, "Holmes!" but apart from the roaring wind, there was nothing. Filled with the fear that I had for ever lost my friend, I went as fast as possible along the slippery path, regardless of my pain or of the wretched ground. Then I was at last there where our prisoner and Holmes had both fallen. With the lantern I could see that the ground was wet and strewn with ferns and moss-covered stones. The sloping ground was a strip, about 20 feet wide, and then the cliff fell vertically to the sea and rocks below. Again, I shouted as loudly as my strength could muster: "Holmes!

Again there was nothing beyond the stormy wind, and yet…. There, in truth, was the faint voice of my friend: "Here, Watson … here below you."

I cannot begin to describe to you the relief and thankfulness I felt, as I realised, I had heard his voice. More than relieved, I called down: "I'm coming, Holmes. … I'm coming, just hold on." I put the lantern aside, as it was in my way, and lay on my stomach flat on the ground. Then I moved slowly, wriggling towards the abyss. I repeatedly stretched out my hands, and tried to go towards Holmes' voice, as he repeatedly called me. Suddenly my hand reached out into nothing. I was at the edge of the cliff. In front of me were torn and broken ferns, and it seemed clear that these marked Holmes' attempts to find a hold. I would have to lift him back over the cliff edge, but for that I would need a firm grip on something solid. I ran my hand through the tangled ferns, and suddenly felt a sharp rock. Was it strong enough to hold our weight? I couldn't tell, but who could tell how long Holmes could hang on in the cliff, with whatever hold he had? I set my doubts aside, laid my right hand over the sharp stone and reached down with my left hand to where I hoped he was. Again I shouted, into the gusting wind: "Take hold of my hand, Holmes!"

At once I felt the iron grip of my friend's hand, as it closed around my wrist. That meant I could close my left hand around his wrist, and pulled with all my strength. Slowly, Holmes' head appeared above the brink of the cliff. Although he was not heavily built, I felt that hundredweights hung on my arm. My shoulder, also irreparably injured in the second Afghan War by a Jezail-ball, fought back against me and the effort. And my right hand, holding fast on the rock, was torn and burning. I knew that the sharp edge of the rock had torn and cut my fingers, and I could feel my blood running down my arm. My heart was hammering, and my breath was harsh and straining. But nothing seemed important except the one thought, that I would not let him go! Now he was so far able, with his free hand, to take a hold on my upper arm. Two more strong pulls, and he could lift both legs over the edge and roll back with me to relative safety in the ferns. We were both gasping with the exertion, side by side, unable to speak for some time. Then we had to crawl on hands and knees, painfully, slowly and carefully, back from the edge.

As we reached the coastal path, we sat for some minutes on the stone slab, which filled almost the whole way. The lantern, which I had put aside earlier, gave a poor light, but even so it was frightful to see how wet, muddy and dishevelled we both were. Now that we were out of mortal danger, I felt the doctor, which I was, taking over, and so I asked Holmes with concern, "Have you any injuries from the fall, Holmes?"

"No, I think not, Watson", he answered thoughtfully, and stood up carefully, to rub and feel himself on body and limbs, before saying: "It seems all is complete and in order, but what about you, old friend, how are you?" As he asked, he looked at my hand and arm, now covered in blood. "That is nothing to worry about, Holmes, it looks worse than it is," I replied, and took my pocket-handkerchief, to bind my hand, at least provisionally. When I had finished, I also tried to stand up. I was grateful for Holmes' outstretched hand.

The coastal path still demanded all our caution, and so it was a slow, silent walk down to the village, each reaching out a hand where needed. Further down below the path the way continued on stone blocks, and we were able, despite our fatigue and weakness, to move more easily. I could already see the harbour, in part because there seemed to be torches burning everywhere. By the burning torchlight I could see that quite in contrast to our arrival earlier, there were now many persons at the quay. Holmes obviously shared my thoughts, for he stopped, looked carefully and spoke with interest: "Something seems to be happening down there. Perhaps a boat has been torn from its moorings in the storm. But we will soon find out. Do you see that man who has left the group and coming towards us waving?"

"Do you think he is waving to us, Holmes?" "That seems quite certain, because there is surely no-one before us or behind us on this path tonight. But before we reach him, I want to tell you that I had in no way and at no time reckoned that our adventure would end like this. It was nevertheless ill-conceived. I have been very remiss."

Holmes was now silent, and I felt I had to reassure him in my own way. "Holmes, you need feel no remorse over the death of Osborn. He had to be bound, so that we were sure that he could not attempt to get away. What followed was regrettable, but an accident for which you were certainly not responsible. And as for his crimes, we have his own complete confession. Furthermore, we both know that he would never have survived long enough to hear the judgment of a court."

I could say no more, for Holmes interrupted me. "Dear friend, I know all that, and you may be assured that it has occupied me. What fills me with remorse, is my guilt towards you, of which I am acutely conscious." Confused, I looked at him, as he continued: "To rescue me you have put yourself in a position of acute and mortal danger. For this selfless act, I can only thank you from the depths of my heart. But it remains so, that it was my irresponsible behaviour which put you in that terrible position."

Holmes' words moved me deeply. I had to answer him, and said: "I had to help you, and I did it gladly, Holmes. If I had to, I would do it again. And that it all would come to this, you could not have foreseen."

Holmes looked at me searchingly, and I saw how first how his tormented expression relaxed, and then, how a smile came to his lips as he remarked, "What you have done was not only to save my life, but also to demonstrate something of which you had yourself doubted." Puzzled by this, I looked at him and he continued: "During our journey from Minions to Liskeard, you told me that you could be never be any help to me, and I said to you that I would wish, in a real emergency, to have no better comrade at my side than you, old friend."

Greatly touched by these words of Holmes, spoken so frankly, I could find no reply. And before I had again collected myself, the man had reached us who had waved from far off. It was indeed the Reverend Gibbs, whose acquaintance we had first made only hours ago, and who now came up to us out of breath and agitated: "Mr. Holmes, Dr. Watson, what has happened? You are soaked through and through. Did old Tonkin shut you out to bear the worst of the storm?"

Before I could answer, Holmes had already replied: "We found Mr Tonkin dead in the cellar of the Anchor. It seems he...." But Holmes could say no more, before Reverend Gibbs interrupted him with the words: "May God have mercy on his poor soul, and grant him eternal peace." Holmes, somewhat surprised, waited and then continued: "It seems he had fallen down the ladder to the cellar."

"No wonder, that the old drunkard should come to such an end; but one should not speak ill of the dead. In the morning I will send one or two persons up to the Inn to bring down the body. And then I will no doubt find a few suitable words to say at his burial"

Before the Vicar could continue, Holmes continued; "As we were finding our way down again in the darkness, we missed our footing and were near to falling over the cliff. We would really be most grateful, if you could recommend a house in the village where we could wash and then find sleep for the night."

Obviously troubled for us, and then kindly, if somewhat cautiously, the vicar had followed Holmes' explanation and answered: "Then thank God that you have suffered nothing worse, gentlemen. You may naturally come to the vicarage, and you will be heartily welcome, as my guests, to sleep there. But we have urgent work to do. I wanted to ask your help, Dr Watson, but after the shock you have suffered, it is perhaps not right that I do so..."

Now it was my turn to interrupt this good man, the vicar of Gorran Haven. "Why, Rev. Gibbs, how can I be of service to you?"

"Just two hours ago, at the height of the storm, a ship ran aground, on the reef by the harbour mouth. Some of our seamen went out, despite the storm, as indeed they always do, to try to reach the capsized vessel. But before they could reach it, the stricken ship broke up, the waves came up over her, and she was lost. A number of the crew were thrown overboard and several of them could be brought out alive. We brought the shipwrecked, as we have so often, into the church where they could be warm and fed, and where we can give them dry clothes. Some of them have injuries, and as I saw you coming down from the cliff I hoped you might be able to see to them, Dr. Watson."

"Naturally, I will of course look at the injured, Rev. Gibbs, but not at once. First I must wash myself clean, and something warm to eat will also help," I replied, and soon I was entering the church. Holmes in the meantime went, at my urging, with the vicar, also to dry, to wash, to take a light meal and then to find the sleep which even his constitution now sorely needed.

As I had already described from first seeing the tower, the church in Gorran Haven is built like a fortress on the cliff above the harbour. The grey granite walls seem to defy the force of nature despite the exposed position. As I entered the church, I saw in the candlelight how simply and unpretentiously this church had been built. The roof, however, was masterly, and resembled an inverted boat over the nave, where only the planking seemed to be lacking. The injured seamen had been laid on the pews on the right-hand side. Mercifully, as a rapid inspection showed, the injuries were in most cases superficial. I could treat them at once. My practiced hands made light work of washing out the wounds, binding them up, and laying splints on one or two fractures. As these patients were taken care of, and so could rest more peacefully, my own tension suddenly fell away. I felt again hunger, and a leaden tiredness fell upon me, After a last look at the exhausted shipwrecked sailors, who, either on the floor or on the hard pews, had mostly at once fallen asleep, I left the church, and with my last strength found my way to the vicarage again. The bed which the vicar offered was thankfully gained and I slept at once.

Conclusions

A steel-blue sky and warm sunshine, and a quiet, calm sea, greeted us as we next morning slipped out of Gorran Haven on the tide. As the steam launch, Veritas, which Lord Robartes had so thoughtfully arranged to be at our disposal, left the harbour, I took a last look back at the tiny fishing village and the surrounding steep cliffs. A cold shiver ran down my spine as I thought of the fearful moments which we had endured last night, but then, by an effort of will, I put these thoughts behind me and followed Holmes into the cabin.

I would not tax your patience any further, dear reader, by describing in great detail our return journey to Lanhydrock. I would simply mention that before the Veritas set course for her home port, Captain Brooke brought us to Fowey, whence Holmes sent a telegram to Lord Robartes, to tell him of our planned arrival. After a light lunch in the station restaurant we took the train to Lostwithiel, from where the Great Western Railway again took us back to Bodmin Road. Here Mr. Jenkins was already waiting for us, and we enjoyed his carriage back to Lanhydrock. There we could go at once to our rooms, and there rest for a moment from our journey, before dressing for dinner.

As I then later entered the inner hall, I found Holmes already waiting there. He was sitting on a window seat in the bay window. His attention was however not directed to the geometrically laid out gardens, nor to the impressive gatehouse. I found him immersed in an article in the newspaper. Something had obvious aroused his interest. As I approached, I saw that it was the issue of The Times of that day. But before I could see what was reported, and on which he had so fixed his attention, he folded the newspaper and stood up, as Lord and Lady Robartes had entered the room behind me. We were greeted heartily and, as Lord Robartes' expression was a guide, he was eagerly awaiting news of our experiences during the last few days. Nevertheless he said clearly: "I am greatly looking forward to your presentation of your enquiries, gentlemen, and even more to the conclusions which you have drawn. But this is not something we should discuss over dinner, and certainly not in the presence of a lady." With these words he smiled affectionately to his wife, and offered her his arm to lead her into the dining room, upon which Holmes and I turned and followed them.

When dinner was over, we gathered as we had a few days earlier, in the smoking room. When we were comfortably provided with whisky and our tobacco, Holmes started his account of our experiences. He did so chronologically, omitting no details, and recounting his conclusions as he had reached them at the end of each stage. Lord Robartes hung on his words, and appeared to be reliving the experiences through the power of his own imagination. So it was that I saw, in Lord Robartes' face, the horror which filled him as Holmes described the discovery of Pascoe's body in the engine house. And when Holmes described Osborn's fatal fall, and then added that he came within a hair's breadth of suffering the same fate, Lord Robartes' expression showed his fear, but then his relief, that it had come out otherwise. As Holmes described how he had been rescued, Lord Robartes turned, to direct to me a look which clearly reflected his recognition and respect of my action. I had to lower my eyes and appear to seek something in my notebook. I was relieved when he turned back and again gave his full attention to Holmes, who had now reached the end of his account. "What an extraordinary adventure you have had to suffer, gentlemen! I am most relieved, that you have come out of it all safe and sound. But

Mr. Holmes, please tell me what you would intend to do next?"

There was a pause, and then Holmes answered thoughtfully. "In the cases of both Samuel Snell and of Jack Tonkin, it will be assumed that these were deaths resulting from accidental causes. Concerning Reginald Dunstan, his death is indeed a consequence of his being over-excited, when he was known to have a weak heart. Certainly, the excitement was a result of the unexpected appearance of Mr. Osborn, but finally, the cause of his heart attack will not be of public interest. There remains thus only the death of Willoughby Pascoe which will be recognised as murder. As I have however already suggested, the local police will, I suspect attempt to explain it elsewhere, and the search for a guilty person will soon be abandoned. Should however an innocent person be charged, we have the handwritten and signed confession of Osborn. When we consider all these aspects, Lord Robartes, I would personally argue that we should now let the whole affair rest. Nevertheless, how we should now proceed must be your decision."

Lord Robartes looked at my friend with surprise. Holmes hastened to explain. "You invited me to make enquiries on your behalf, and I did so, although this subsequent matter could not then be your concern. You needed to be sure that your own plans, concerning the foundation-stone-laying for your charitable foundation, were not threatened by any unpleasant surprise. It was thus your wish for clarification of the disturbing events which had earlier occurred, which led me to the series of murders which Mr Osborn had committed." Lord Robartes followed these words most carefully. It took some moments before he was ready to reply, but then he spoke decisively and with authority. "I am entirely in agreement with you, Mr. Holmes. Who would benefit by bringing this whole business to public attention? No-one! Mr. Osborn can no longer be called to account for his crimes. The ordered and quiet life of Mrs. Ruth Lang, the sister of Mr. Osborn, would on the other hand be seriously disturbed. Her childhood was already difficult enough; I would now wish to spare here the confrontation with her brother's crimes. As far as she knows, her brother died long ago, lost at sea. I consider that it is wiser to let it rest there." I had listened with great respect to these words of Lord Robartes, and, as I nodded my agreement, I felt my heart filled with warm satisfaction, that I had nor erred in my judgment of Lord Robartes, nor indeed of Holmes. These were men of most noble character!

It was Lord Robartes himself who broke the long silence, which inevitably followed his decision. "And now, gentlemen, after so much tension and anxiety, I am sure that you would benefit from a few days' relaxation. May I invite you remain at Lanhydrock, and to be my guests at the planned foundation stone ceremony at the weekend?"

"Thank you for your most gracious invitation, Lord Robartes. However, I must decline, for I cannot permit myself a longer absence from London at this time. I really must return tomorrow", replied Holmes. His answer did not surprise me, for I knew that as soon as a case was solved, Holmes' interest in it, and in the details involved, quickly diminished. Apart from that, I had a suspicion that he had, when reading The Times, discovered something which had caught his attention and curiosity. But now Lord Robartes turned to me, interrupting my thoughts by asking: "And you, Dr. Watson, what would you say? Can your patients wait a little longer for your return?" I did not at once reply, for I must admit that the thought of a few days enjoying the hospitality of Lord Robartes, and meeting personally William Gladstone, one of the great politicians of our time, was very tempting. As far as my practice was concerned, my neighbour, Dr. Smythe, could surely represent me for a day or two more. But that night on the cliffs at Gorran Haven had yet again reminded me, how vulnerable is our existence. The awareness of the fragility of our happiness, and of the vulnerability of our familiar everyday life, had again been brought home to me. And thus I had chosen to return to that place where my heart would again find calm.

"I regret, Lord Robartes, that I must, as did my friend, decline your generous invitation. Not only is it the thought of my patients which dictates my reply, but much more, that of my dear wife, who is most certainly eagerly awaiting my safe return." A momentary disappointment crossed Lord Robartes face, but then he smiled in understanding, and replied: "Dr. Watson, love is surely the most valuable gift which God has given us. I understand completely your decision – but you will, gentlemen, at least perhaps accord me this evening the pleasure of a game of billiards together." "But gladly, Lord Robartes", replied Holmes, and I readily agreed.

On the way to the billiards room, Lord Robartes and Holmes were already engaged in an agitated discussion over variations of the game, and about different properties and qualities of wood for the manufacture of cues. I was amused by this expert conversation, to which I would surely add little. I entered the billiards room behind them. And yet, as the door closed behind me, I already felt how the tension and fatigue of these last days fell away from me, and I knew that the Cornwall affair had truly found its conclusion.

End

Lightning Source UK Ltd.
Milton Keynes UK
UKHW010650050221
378300UK00001B/32

9 781787 055490